Judicial Punishment in England

Dr J. A. Sharpe is a Senior Lecturer in History at the University of York. His publications include *Defamation and Sexual Slander in Early Modern England: The Church Courts at York* (1980), *Crime in Seventeenth-century England* (1983), and *Crime and the Law in English Satirical Prints 1600–1832* (1986).

in the same series

Wealth and Inequality in Britain
W. D. Rubinstein

The Government of Space
Alison Ravetz

Educational Opportunity and Social Change in England
Michael Sanderson

A Property-owning Democracy?
M. J. Daunton

Sport in Britain
Tony Mason

The Labour Movement in Britain
John Saville

The Voluntary Impulse
Frank Prochaska

British Welfare Policy
Anne Digby

JUDICIAL PUNISHMENT IN ENGLAND

J. A. Sharpe

faber and faber
LONDON · BOSTON

First published in 1990
by Faber and Faber Limited
3 Queen Square London WC1N 3AU

Phototypeset by Wilmaset, Birkenhead, Wirral
Printed in Great Britain by
Richard Clay Ltd, Bungay, Suffolk

A CIP record for this book is available from the British Library

ISBN 0-571-14060-2

HISTORICAL HANDBOOKS

It is widely recognized that many of the problems of present-day society are deeply rooted in the past, but the actual lines of historical development are often known only to a few specialists, while the policy-makers and analysts themselves frequently rely on a simplified, dramatized, and misleading version of history. Just as the urban landscape of today was largely built in a world that is no longer familiar, so the policy landscape is shaped by attitudes and institutions formed under very different conditions in the past. This series of specially commissioned handbooks aims to provide short, up-to-date studies in the evolution of current problems, not in the form of narratives but as critical accounts of the ways in which the present is formed by the past, and of the roots of present discontents. Designed for those with little time for extensive reading in the specialized literature, the books contain full bibliographies for further study. The authors aim to be as accurate and comprehensive as possible, but not anodyne; their arguments, forcefully expressed, make the historical experience available in challenging form, but do not presume to offer ready-made solutions.

Contents

	Preface	ix
I	Introduction	1
II	The Old Penal Regime	18
	Early Modern Punishment: An Overview	19
	The Rise and Fall of Capital Punishment	27
	The Search for Secondary Punishments	36
III	The Nineteenth Century	50
	The Hulks and Transportation	51
	The Prison	61
	The Wider Perspective	75
IV	The Twentieth Century	88
	An Age of Optimism	89
	The Abolition of Capital Punishment	100
	Towards the Crisis	109
V	Conclusion	124
	Notes	132
	Bibliography	139
	Index	146

Preface

The bulk of the work upon which this book is based was carried out in the British Library, the British Library of Political and Economic Science, and the J. B. Morrell Library of the University of York. I am grateful to all of these institutions and their staffs.

It should be stressed that my subject is developments in England, or, after they were brought together in official statistics, England and Wales. Northern Ireland and Scotland currently have their own prison systems, while for earlier periods further complications are presented by the fact that Scotland had (and indeed still has) an independent legal system, and that the operation of that system has so far been little investigated in its historical dimension. Writing a book of this type on Britain as a whole would not, therefore, be a realistic undertaking at present. However, the decision to take 1550 as a starting point has, it is to be hoped, added a chronological breadth to the book. I have long sensed a feeling implicit among sociologists and criminologists that, in crime and punishment as in so much else, the world before about 1750 was more or less static, and thus not really worth detailed analysis. I hope that this book will, if nothing else, modify this illusion.

J. A. Sharpe, York
January 1990

I

Introduction

Our judicial system is punishing a lot of people these days. This is, of course, in large measure a consequence of the fact that a lot of people are committing crimes.[1] In 1986, the most recent year for which figures are available as I write, the police in England and Wales were aware of some 3,800,000 notifiable offences, 7 per cent more than in 1985. A total of 521,000 offenders were found guilty or cautioned for indictable offences, while another 520,000 non-motoring offenders were found guilty on summary conviction at magistrates' courts. There were also about 1,100,000 motoring offenders, many of whom would receive written warnings or fixed penalties rather than be prosecuted. If crime is one of the most familiar problems which our society faces, punishing those committing it is obviously one of the most constant activities of government.

As might be imagined, the range of fates awaiting those found guilty of committing a crime is varied. A large number of such people, indeed, are not 'punished' at all in the layman's meaning of the term. In 1986, 214,000 offenders were cautioned by the police, that is, they were given a formal warning after having admitted a criminal offence which could have led to prosecution. Another 18,300 were given an absolute discharge, and 78,000 a conditional discharge. A further 42,400 were put on probation. Others, mainly juvenile offenders, were placed under one of a number of types of order: attendance centre orders, detention centre orders, and so on. Some 1,500 went into care, and another 21,100 into youth custody. A further 30,900, most of them adults, received a fully suspended sentence, and 3,900 a partially suspended one. By far the most common penalty, however, was fining: 1,580,000 persons, including the bulk of motoring offenders, were fined. Further inroads into the pockets of offenders were made by compensation orders, which can be imposed with or without other punishment, by which offenders make direct recompense to their victims: 3,200 such orders were made at the crown courts, 94,000 at the magistrates' courts.

Imprisonment, although in terms of the number of offenders it deals with coming far behind fining in statistical importance, is the form of punishment which attracts most attention in modern Britain, and is the one which is probably equated by most people with 'real' punishment. The Prison Services report for 1986–7 revealed that the service at that time was responsible for some 140 establishments, and breaking them down into categories reminds us that 'prison' has become a generic term for a wide range of institutions. There were 26 local prisons for men; 38 closed training centres for men; 10 open training prisons for men; 18 remand centres for males; 23 closed youth custody centres for male offenders; 8 open youth custody centres for male offenders; 8 senior detention centres for young male offenders; 4 junior detention centres for young male offenders; 1 local prison (Holloway) for women; 4 other closed prisons for women; 3 open prisons for women; 3 remand centres for women and girls; 2 closed youth custody centres for girls; 2 open youth custody centres for girls. The report also listed 16 new establishments or units under construction, and noted that there were 12 more establishments or units at the design stage. The report also noted that running the system in 1986–7 involved the efforts of 28,182 men and women, of whom 19,072 were prison officers.

The carceral institutions already in being are not short of inmates, and, if current trends continue, there is no reason to suppose that those currently planned or already under construction will be so when they are completed. The average daily population of those institutions under the control of the prison service in 1986 was 46,900, with a maximum of 48,400 at the end of December. These inmates were fitted into certified normal accommodation, as of 30 June, of 40,811. Of receptions into these institutions, 55,469 were suspects awaiting trial, 16,128 were convicted unsentenced prisoners, 86,153 were prisoners under sentence, and 3,665 were non criminal prisoners, the largest single category of these last being held under the Immigration Act. The length of sentence varied. Of those sentenced at the magistrates' court, where the maximum sentence is six months, 41 per cent of males and 46 per cent of females were sentenced to two months or less. Of those sentenced by the crown courts, 29 per cent of male prisoners and 41 per cent of females were sentenced to less than six months; 28 per cent and 26 per cent respectively to between six and twelve months; 50 per cent of males and 30 per cent of females to between one and four years; and 12 per cent of males and 4 per cent of females to four years or more. Of remand prisoners, including both those awaiting trial and those convicted but unsentenced, an estimated 700 had been in prison for between six and twelve months, and about 100 for over twelve months.

This machinery of punishment costs a good deal of money. Costing the global impact of crime and crime control on the national economy is obviously a difficult business, not least because so many crimes go unreported. Taking the United Kingdom as a whole, however, it has been calculated that for 1984–5 crime absorbed £5,805,000,000 worth of resources from the public sector, and £2,655,000,000 from the private sector.[2] As in any year, a proportion of this sum would go to meet the costs of punishment. So far little has been done by way of estimating the costs (let alone the cost effectiveness) of punishment, although an important pioneering study revealed a number of interesting points:[3] a thirteen-month probation order, for example, cost the same as keeping a prisoner in gaol for a month while at about the same time the fines raised by magistrates' courts were making that part of the system virtually self-sufficient. But it is the cost of keeping the prison service going which catches public attention most forcefully. Although dwarfed by health, education and defence expenditure, the total cost of the prison service, £786,500,000 for England and Wales in 1986–7, is substantial enough. The largest single element of this sum was pay, allowances and superannuation for prison officers, £365,954,000 of the total manpower costs of £512,906,000. Inmate related costs came to £40,776,000, of which £16,076,000 was spent on victualling prisoners, and £11,774,000 on clothing and equipment for them. The administrative costs of the service's headquarters and its regional offices was £50,100,000. Put differently, in 1986 it cost an average £252 to keep a prisoner in his or her cell for a week. Average weekly earnings for an adult in full time employment that year were £181.20, by way of contrast.

All of this would be much less worrying if we could convince ourselves that the system of punishment was having any effect: or, to be more precise (for, as we shall argue, there is considerable lack of clarity as to what the 'effects' of punishment are meant to be) if it was reducing crime. Every year more crimes, on the strength of the judicial statistics, are committed, so in terms of general deterrence our current methods of punishment could be portrayed as defective. And although it is difficult given the different types of custodial institution and other forms of punishment to argue from overall rates of recidivism, the presence of habitual criminals and recurrent offenders seems to suggest that a substantial proportion of those experiencing punishment are not deterred from committing further crimes. Largely owing to such considerations, punishment of criminals is currently a subject of continual discussion, among politicians, in the media, and more generally. Arguably, this discussion, and our grasp of our current situation, would benefit from an exploration of the historical dimensions of the subject, not least because the state of affairs in which we currently find ourselves is so often contrasted to some supposed previous state where the criminal was kept in check more effectively by a different (and usually harsher) penal regime.

The subject of this book is, therefore, the history of judicial punishment in England, the period it covers being from about the middle of the sixteenth century to the present day. As will be appreciated, trying to recount this history in the compass of a short essay of this type is a daunting proposition. But the task will be made easier and perhaps more worthwhile if we pause for an initial consideration of what the objectives of judicial punishment might be on a theoretical level. It should be stressed from the outset that it is judicial punishment with which we shall be concerned. Other forms of punishment existed and still do exist. For much of the period with which we shall deal, for example, employers had rights of corporal and other forms of punishment over their apprentices and domestic servants, while schoolteachers had similar rights over their pupils. Such forms of punishment are not our concern. Neither are such random acts of 'punishment' as lynching or other expressions of popular action, or the rather more numerous examples which history affords of official actions such as the shooting down of rioters or the summary execution of rebels in the wake of an uprising. In the context of this book, punishment means the infliction of a legally defined or a legally acceptable penalty imposed by a legally accredited authority upon a criminally responsible person who has, after due legal process, been found guilty of breaking the law.

That those in positions of authority have been willing to inflict such punishment, and have, in fact, often seen it as their duty to do so, was a demonstrable fact long before the starting point of this study. Broadly, as the power of the monarch (or, more abstractly the state) increased over the middle ages, the right of the royal courts to adjudicate criminal and civil suits became more marked. The story is a complex one, and we must be cautious in accepting any oversimplified or unilinear developmental model: yet it is difficult, whatever the underlying complexities, not to accept the conventional account of the broad developments. There was the gradual encroachment of central upon local power, the downgrading of local law codes in favour of the royal law, the gradual replacement of the feud by the royal court as the accepted means of dispute resolution. It was, perhaps, this last development which is the most relevant to the history of judicial punishment. It gradually became accepted that private vengeance for an offence or injury should be replaced by the collective vengeance of the king's justice. Crime, to adopt the modern terminology, was an offence against society (as represented by the royal law) as well as against the individual.[4] Anthropologists have demonstrated that in the simple societies they study the feud can be a rather more complex phenomenon than some historians have imagined, while they have also shown that small-scale human societies can operate without a law enforcement system in our sense of the term.[5] Yet by 1550, perhaps to a greater extent in England than in some other states, western Europeans were used to looking to the legal system for settling their disputes, and were accustomed to the notion that what we would describe as crimes might appropriately be dealt with by courts which would inflict punishments upon the persons convicted of committing them.

But even by that date it is obvious that there were varying ideas of what the punishment of criminals was meant to achieve. This confusion is still with us: and we must accordingly set out at least a basic statement of what people consider the functions of judicial punishment to be. In so doing we must, of course, sometimes compress very complex arguments into very simple formats. A wide variety of people, from Immanuel Kant to the more thoughtful modern prison officer, have reflected on this issue, and to do full justice to the fruits of this reflection would lead to a consideration of ethical and philosophical matters which are largely irrelevant to this book, and issues of criminological or social policy which for reasons of space must be excluded from it. Even so, our later discussion of historical developments can only be strengthened and clarified if we devote a few pages to exploring the main theoretical positions regularly adopted in any debate on the punishment of crime. Broadly speaking, there are three such: those which lay emphasis respectively upon the deterrent, the reformative, or the retributive aspects of judicial punishment.[6]

Deterrence is probably the most frequently deployed argument in favour of judicial punishment. The fundamental thinking behind deterrence is a very simple one: the knowledge that an illegal act or type of behaviour will be punished inhibits potential criminals in any desire which they might have to commit such acts, while an individual who has experienced punishment inflicted for an illegal action will feel inhibited from committing further illegalities. The underpinning notion is that human beings are rational entities who seek pleasure and avoid pain. Confronted by deterrent punishment at its most vivid, in the form of the public execution or the rotting corpse of the gibbeted criminal, rational people would be bound to be dissuaded from emulating the behaviour which invites such a fate. By the mid eighteenth century Enlightenment thinkers were increasingly revolted by such spectacles, and were developing a more sophisticated view of the nature of deterrence. The idea was now to impose a system of penalties, each of them a known and certain reward for a different type of crime. In addition, a number of thinkers (Cesare Beccaria being perhaps the most frequently cited of them) were becoming convinced that deterrence worked better on the basis of a certainty of punishment: it was more effective to catch a larger proportion of criminals and inflict a lesser punishment upon them than to attempt to deter by the spectacular and barbaric punishment of a smaller proportion. Even the most avid proponents of deterrence have been unlikely to claim that it deters everybody. Nevertheless, the notion of deterrence as one of the major objectives of judicial punishment has an attractively common-sense feel to it, and is still regularly adduced as a major force in justifying punishment.

Any simplistic notions of the value of deterrent punishments must, however, be modified by two considerations of a more or less ethical nature. The first is the concept of proportionality, the idea that even if a punishment is intended to deter, there should be some sort of equivalence between the gravity of the crime in question and the gravity of the punishment to be inflicted. If we take the deterrence model to a *reductio ad absurdum*, it would be possible to support the view that if the death penalty deters, it will be able to deter not only murderers, but also shoplifters, and might therefore be applied to this latter category of offenders. Indeed, in the early nineteenth century, defenders of the legal status quo were arguing that abolishing the death penalty for shoplifting would lead to a collapse in respect for property and a more general anarchy. Furthermore, given that shoplifting is more likely to be a premeditated crime than homicide, a case could easily be made for arguing that a strong deterrent punishment would be a good way of cutting the incidence of the former offence. Yet it seems likely that any attempt to introduce the death penalty on these grounds in present day Britain would not prosper: public opinion would not see it as a proportionate punishment. Secondly, the proponent of deterrence has to accept the basic proposition that persons being punished have to be guilty of the offence for which they suffer. Again, taking the deterrent position to one of its possible logical conclusions, it does not much matter if a few of those being punished for a crime are innocent: if the role of imprisonment is to deter potential offenders, the fact that a few of those imprisoned are innocent is neither here nor there. Such a conclusion, it is to be hoped, would be unacceptable:

yet the point does indicate another modification which must be built into any deterrent model.

The deterrent approach is, moreover, subject to a number of practical difficulties. The most salient of these is that, despite the idea having been entrenched in our thinking on crime control since at least the sixteenth century, we have very little evidence of the extent to which deterrence works or the ways in which it does so. As we have noted, even the most optimistic proponent of deterrence would be unlikely to argue that all potential offenders would be deterred. Indeed, as current figures suggest, the degree to which the punishments currently at our disposal fail to deter those experiencing them from further lawbreaking is far from reassuring. The reasons for this are varied. Perhaps the most obvious, as far as our current situation is concerned, is that the modern prison, despite its intrinsic nastiness, is as likely to act as a school for crime as a deterrent against it. But even in the age before imprisonment in the modern sense, the public execution, the public pillory, and the public gibbeting of criminals, all of them spectacular demonstrations that crime did not pay, also failed to deter. Evidence given to the 1866 Royal Commission on Capital Punishment included a statement by a prison chaplain to the effect that of the 167 persons under sentence of death to whom he had ministered, 164 had attended at least one public execution. The central problem, perhaps, is that human beings, and certainly most criminal ones, do not calculate their chances of obtaining pain and pleasure as rationally as would the eighteenth-century *philosophe*, or if they do, they arrive at rather different answers: the point is illustrated by the eighteenth-century English criminal, who, while awaiting execution, commented that, 'there are so many chances *for* us, and so few against us, that I never thought of it coming to this.'[7] Moreover, one of the gaping holes in the evidence needed to support the deterrence argument is the lack of any substantial body of studies of people who do *not* commit crimes. We have numerous studies of criminals: yet our understanding of deterrence might well be deepened by some research on people who are not.

Such studies, one suspects, would reveal that fear of punishment is just one of a variety of factors inhibiting people from criminal conduct. That most inhabitants of this country do not steal is probably not the outcome of their having acquired a detailed knowledge of the punishments for stealing as set out in the 1968 Theft Act. The generally held awareness that stealing, if detected, might lead to a criminal conviction and imprisonment undoubtedly acts as an inhibition. Yet socialization, the early inculcation of a sense of right and wrong, and the subsequent acceptance of the moral code upon which society rests, are probably far more important. This is not to retreat into some sort of neo-anarchist argument that society can exist without a state apparatus, as human beings instinctively recognize that their true interests lie in maintaining responsible social attitudes: without fear of judicial punishment, a proportion of normally law-abiding people would doubtless commit crimes. It is merely to argue that a simple model of deterrence is far too mechanical. One of the reasons why law-abiding citizens do not break the law is that they fear the consequences of being caught and punished for so doing: but it is not the only reason.

Deterrence, then, is one of the classic objectives of punishment. Another, increasingly familiar from the early nineteenth century onwards, is the reformation of the criminal. The bases of this model are varied. One of the oldest, perhaps, is the fundamental Christian proposition that all human beings have something worth saving within them. More prosaically, there is the notion, which flowered in the first half of the nineteenth century, that crime is a 'social problem', and that social problems are there to be solved. Hence the heightening of the desire to reform the criminal after about 1800 can be interpreted as one facet of that broader impulse which also wished to provide proper urban drainage, enforce factory acts, keep child labour out of coal mines, and so on. On a more strictly practical level, the more hard-headed of the 'punishment as reformation' school could argue with some force that there is a considerable logic in accepting that since most offenders undergoing punishment will eventually return to society (many, indeed, never leave it) it makes sense so to work upon offenders that they will not return to crime. To this end, and taking the analogy of crime with disease, some have argued that the criminal should be treated, rather than punished. Thus in most developed states the great work of law enforcement embraces not only policemen, prison officers and judges but also social workers, psychologists, and probation officers.

As we have suggested, the rise of the idea of reforming the criminal is involved with a broader change in the view of how the state might impinge upon the individual. It is also connected with a certain idea of the nature of crime: it presupposes that crime might not simply be a moral issue, arising from the individual's inability to distinguish between right and wrong, but that medical, psychological, and above all social factors might also be involved. Of course, although the idea of reformation really arrived around 1800, it can be traced at much earlier periods: it can be seen in the classical world, and was present at the beginning of the period covered by this book in some of the thinking about the role of houses of correction. The ideal of reformation has a respectable pedigree, and a number of writers have recognized its virtues. The most attractive of these to modern thinkers, and certainly the one which connects the ideal to the nineteenth century, is the way in which reformation of criminals has generally been regarded as a progressive project. As Sir Walter Moberley commented:

> The truisms of one generation of legislators and administrators have become baseless and grotesque illusions in the eye of their successors. What was scorned not so long ago as wildly utopian and hare-brained has now become settled and avowed official policy.[8]

The reformative ideal does, at least, give some hope that crime might be diminished, if not actually overcome.

The idea of reforming the criminal, of the solution to the crime problem resting in treatment rather than punishment, is one which has received considerable criticism, much of it, as might be imagined, from persons of a conservative or right-wing persuasion. One basic issue is that the treatment model diminishes the individual's responsibility for his or her actions: the criminal does not commit crime through being evil, but rather as a consequence of being socially deprived, psychologically disturbed, or whatever. A second problem with the reformation model is that its proponents often have a simplistic hostility to more traditional models of punishment, writing them off as vestiges of a barbaric past which will fade as humanitarianism and rationality advance. Further problems with reformation revolve around the fear that treatment might prove to be as restrictive and damaging to the offender's rights as are the older forms of punishment (the Soviet practice of placing political dissidents in institutions for the mentally ill comes readily to mind). Thus C. S. Lewis argued in 1946 that

> The things done to the criminal, even if they are called cures, will be just as compulsory as they were in the old days when we called them punishments . . . My contention is that this doctrine, merciful though it appears, really means that each one of us, from the moment he breaks the law, is deprived of the rights of a human being.[9]

Certainly, arguing from the extreme example of the totalitarian state, it can be understood how attempts to 'cure' offenders might lead to official denial of their status as rational beings worthy of full citizenship.

In democratic Britain, the number of stages through which the habitual offender passes, and the number of specialists which he or she will meet *en route*, is daunting. Most offenders will have been seen at various stages by social workers, psychologists, psychiatrists, and probation officers. Habitual offenders begin their experience of punishment with a caution or a conditional discharge, and will end in a long-stay rehabilitative institution after passing through the probation service and various short-stay punitive institutions. Even in a reformatory system, society's early attempts to be helpful end, if the offender will not reform, by becoming punitive and coercive. But this range of institutions and specialists connected to a reforming punishment system reminds us of two basic points. The first is that such systems are very expensive. Arguably, no punishment system has ever had enough resources put into it to give it a fair chance of reforming the criminal, yet the fact remains that maintaining the institutions and functionaries demanded by even an imperfect system aiming at reform costs a great deal of money. The second is that, as with deterrence, a strong case could be made for arguing that reformation doesn't work. Despite our extensive and costly system of penal and non-penal institutions designed to 'cure' crime, we are confronted by a high level of recidivism and ever increasing crime rates. And, as we have noted above, in the last resort we still turn to the repression and coercion of those offenders who seem unresponsive to the efforts made to cure them.

Part of the inhibitions which impede the type of imaginative leap required to envisage and operate a fully reformative system lies in the existence of another strand in our thinking about punishment, the retributive one. Despite the claims of many writers, particularly those putting their thoughts on paper when the times favoured optimistic attitudes about punishment, it is clear that, for most people, the idea of retribution is central to thinking about the punishment of criminals. When asked how punishment is justified, a common response is that a guilty act is intrinsically worthy of punishment: before further reflection leads to thoughts of deterrence or reform, the immediate reaction when thinking about punishment is usually a retributive one. To the retributionist, the nature and extent of the punishment meted out to the criminal is based on some estimate of the pain (a term capable of wide definition) which the offender deserves. Criminal punishment is regarded as a necessary expression of society's disgust at and disapprobation of crime. The wider social context within which retribution operates varies: the appropriate retribution for theft, for example, would be viewed differently by an eighteenth-century parliamentarian, his modern equivalent, or a Muslim fundamentalist. There will be the problem, in any cultural context, of determining the exact nature of the punishment which any offence deserves. Yet, in the last resort, the members of most societies which have a developed system of judicial punishment would see revenge against the offender as one of the fundamental objectives of that system. One suspects that emphasis on this point marks one of the most important divergences between the popular and the academic approaches to the problem of judicial punishment.

It should be noted, however, that retribution acts on more than a simplistic 'eye for an eye, tooth for a tooth' level. A number of implications arise from the notion that punishment is in a certain sense deserved: that an evil act should, morally, bring about unpleasant consequences for its perpetrator. The first of these is that the punishment of criminals plays an important part in re-affirming social norms, or what Durkheim called collective sentiments. The knowledge that criminals are being punished makes honest citizens more satisfied about not being criminals. The generation of such sentiments, one suspects, is the most important function of judicial punishment. Secondly, curiously, retribution might well leave the way open for more effective reformation. As D. J. B. Hawkins has put it:

> Reformation, however, is really procured through punishment, when the delinquent person realises that he has deserved his punishment and ought to amend himself accordingly . . . the vice of regarding punishment entirely from the point of view of reformation and deterrence lies precisely in forgetting that a just punishment is deserved.[10]

We return again to the basic premise that individuals do have some responsibility for their actions, a proposition which, however humane a system of treating crime might be developed, should not be lost sight of entirely in a democratic state. The familiar concept of the criminal 'paying his debt to society' does presuppose that there is such a thing as a wider social morality to which the individual has responsibilities. Arguably, one of the objectives of judicial punishment ought to be to clarify offenders' thinking on that point: an offender who is convinced that he or she has done wrong is more likely to reform, or has at least taken an important first step in that direction.

Yet if the deterrent and reformative models of punishment have their drawbacks, so too does the retributive. At its most extreme, as the correspondence columns of the British press regularly demonstrate, it can lead to a downgrading of the convicted criminal: some would regard him as a being entitled, in the classic mid-Victorian formula, to little more than 'hard bed, hard labour, and hard fare'. Criminals, so the argument runs, get what they deserve: all attempts at reformation through non-custodial and custodial means are irrelevant, and prisons themselves should be regarded as little more than dustbins of humanity, within whose walls human refuse is placed in a massive act of containment. The retributive model thus moves towards a sanitizing one. To such arguments, the more sophisticated proponent of retributive punishment would reply that such punishment is not justified merely on some simplistic notion of tit for tat or the infliction of pain for its own sake. There is a moral responsibility to safeguard the convicted criminal while punishment is being inflicted as much as there is to safeguard society by inflicting the punishment. Others have denied the more simplistic notion of the nature of retributive punishment by approaching it from some basic conception of civil rights: thus, in awarding punishment we are recognizing the full citizenship of the punished, treating them as an equal, almost arguing that to be punished for an offence against the law is the sane citizen's right. But here too, the convicted prisoner must still have rights, and among these is the right to be protected against what the framers of the United States Constitution described as 'cruel and unusual punishments'. Most of those currently incarcerated in British gaols are there because they have committed acts which most of us abhor, some of them for having committed acts which would disgust or horrify us. Yet we must accept, however regretfully in some cases, that they are fellow human beings and our fellow citizens, and should be treated as such.

Once more, therefore, we return to the problem of the practical application of a model of punishment. Retribution, we have suggested, enjoys a wide popular currency precisely because it proceeds from a sense of moral indignation: the fact that a person has been convicted of a crime is enough to justify their being made to suffer. But again we encounter the need for proportionality in punishment: the gravity of the suffering inflicted ought to be proportionate to the gravity of the wrong which has been done. It should also be noted that retribution does not exclude the other objectives of punishement. Retributionists would argue that the essence of deterrence lies not in the punishment of the offence, which is retributive, but rather in publicizing it. Even so, the possibility of such publicity being used to deterrent effect would not be denied by the thoughtful retributionist. Neither would the possibility of reforming the offender: it would simply be argued that reformation cannot be achieved by punishment proper, but should be regarded as a secondary objective. Perhaps the main conclusion we should draw from this discussion of basic assumptions about punishment, indeed, is that the three main strands we have delineated are rarely clearly separable on either a theoretical or a practical level. Certainly, debate over crimes or punishment, or social policy more generally, is rarely clear in separating these three themes, or their implications.

The alert reader will already have perceived some omissions from this short and schematic sketch of the approaches to judicial punishment. Perhaps the most vital of these is that, in large measure, considerations of power have so far been neglected. In reality, of course, the criminal law and the punishment of crime do not operate in a social vacuum: rather, they operate in a full social and cultural context, and in a more or less complex interaction with a host of other phenomena. Among these is the problem of where the power to punish is invested, and in whose interests this power operates. In addessing this problem, the use of such terms as 'the state' or 'society' as if they were value-free constants is a practice open to serious criticism. Debate over punishment often involves statements from interested parties about what society needs, or how society should be protected. In such circumstances, one is entitled to ask what exactly 'society' means. A radical answer to this question might well be that in many historical and current situations 'society' serves as a convenient shorthand for powerful or propertied groups within the society in question. Even those who are not radicals should remain open to the evident fact that punishment does reflect certain types of power relationships, the modern reformative model, with its battalions of experts, no less than any other. It is no accident that one of the first essays to attempt to analyse the nature of the criminal law and the punishments it depended upon in eighteenth-century England was written from a Marxist perspective, and firmly integrated such matters into the structure of property ownership and power existing at the time.[11] Connected to these issues, of course, are the much broader ones of the causes of crime, and the relationship of social structure to criminality. Obviously, these issues are of great relevance to the history of punishment: logically, one of the main determinants of the objectives of punishment will be the punishers' perception of why people commit crime. We need not involve ourselves too deeply in these matters, except perhaps to note that the main polarity is provided by what could be described as a 'nature versus nurture' debate: do people commit crimes as a result of inherent wickedness or because of social conditions? Variations in types and objectives of judicial punishment might be expected to follow variations in policy makers' ideas on this matter.

The historian should, therefore, be alert to the possibility of judicial punishment being somehow related to the peculiarities of the social hierarchy or class structure of the society being studied. Further complications are created by the intentionality of the criminal law. In the modern democratic state, arguably, the law is designed primarily to set limits to a certain minimum standard of conduct to which everybody must adhere. This minimum standard changes, this change may be debated, and as a result the law may change. Yet it is clear that the criminal law, as it exists in most modern democratic states, is prescriptive rather than proscriptive: it sets out what will happen to people who park their cars illegally or kill other people. Despite the implied reaffirmation of normative values it makes in so doing, the criminal law leaves the teaching of morality and civic responsibility to other sources. But this situation is less clear in some societies studied by anthropologists, in some totalitarian states, and in some historical contexts. Judicial punishment, therefore, often operates in a context where the affirmation of broader cultural values, whether those of 'society' writ large or of dominant social groups, is of crucial importance.

Approaching the history of punishment, not least over a fairly wide timespan, thus involves confronting a number of complexities. It is hoped that this introduction has at least cleared the ground by opening up, perhaps too resolutely from the perspective of current penal debate, what some of the relevant themes and issues might be. Winston Churchill, when Home Secretary, commented that 'the mood and temper of the public in regard to the treatment of crime and criminals is one of the most unfailing tests of the civilization of any country'.[12] This is, perhaps, something of an exaggeration: it has recently been suggested that in eighteenth-century England, for example, the punishment of criminals was an issue of roughly the same ethical standing as the disposal of sewage.[13] Even so (and setting aside the point that how a society deals with its sewage is a fair indicator of something), it remains clear that how societies punish those breaking their laws might well provide deeper insights into those societies: modern criminals living three to a cell in the chamber pot's stench, or a seventeenth-century felon about to be hanged for horse theft, might well be or have been able to offer a few thoughts in support of Churchill's contention.

II

The Old Penal Regime

Writing the history of punishment in the early modern period involves confronting a number of especially complex difficulties. These, for the most part, operate on three levels. Firstly, before the eighteenth century there is little by way of easily accessible materials from which statistics might be derived. For earlier periods, such statistics have to be abstracted from difficult and fragmented archival sources. Secondly, the modern observer must make a conceptual leap of considerable dimensions in order to appreciate that, however unfamiliar or barbaric pre-industrial punishments may seem, they had their own rationale, and should be analysed in their own terms and within the context of their own period. Thirdly, and again before the eighteenth century, there was surprisingly little by way of public debate on the nature and objectives of punishment. The era of the Civil War and Interregnum (1642–60), a period which saw wide ranging debates on a number of social issues, is a partial exception to this generalization: yet, broadly speaking, before the problem of crime and punishment became a matter of widespread public debate around the middle of the eighteenth century, there was little by way of that public discussion of punishment which is so familiar in the late twentieth century. Usually, it would seem, the criminal law and the penalties it imposed was something which was taken for granted.

Nevertheless, judicial punishment over the period *c.* 1550–1750 demands serious treatment. One of the reasons for studying history (arguably the main reason) is to stretch our imagination by trying to comprehend the variety of ways in which human beings have organized their affairs. The punishment of criminals provides one of the richest areas where this variety can be observed. Early modern punishments might seem distressing and puzzling to the modern observer: on the one hand, the distasteful spectacle of the public execution: on the other, the shaming punishments, tailing off into the rituals of the skimmington, which meant so much in the context of the local community.[1] Yet these, like many other past phenomena which seem so alien today, did not exist devoid of any wider meaning. They were there to serve purposes which, explicitly or otherwise, were felt to be appropriate to the needs of the society in which they flourished. As such, they deserve serious attention.

Early Modern Punishment: An Overview

The most striking feature of judicial punishment in the Elizabethan and Stuart periods was the variety of ways in which it could be inflicted. The sixteenth century had a whole battery of punishments at its disposal. Some of these, like fines, are still with us. Others, like the stocks or the ducking stool, seem very distant. Making sense of these various punishments is difficult, not least because they have previously so often been treated in a purely antiquarian fashion, or simply adduced to illustrate the barbarity of past ages. Three interwoven strands can be discerned in the ideas which underlay them. Firstly, they were usually public: the drunkard placed in the stocks, like the murderer hanged on the gallows, suffered before an audience. Secondly, that audience, especially if we ignore the ceremonies at Tyburn, was drawn overwhelmingly from the local population: geographical mobility in pre-industrial England should not be underrated, yet a resident offender punished in the middle of a village or in the market place of a provincial town suffered in a context where he or she was known and familiar. Thirdly, many of these punishments were designed to shame and, perhaps by shaming, purify offenders and thus pave the way for their reintegration into the moral universe whose code they had transgressed.

Some of these punishments, despite their familiarity in antiquarian works or books of popular history, are difficult to trace in legal records. The branks, a metal mask with a spur to hold the tongue, allegedly much used against scolding women, is rarely noted in court archives. The employment of the ducking stool, a device whereby offenders (again, typically female scolds) were dipped in a pond or stream, is also elusive. In a sixty-year period in Stuart Essex, for example, only one example of the use of the ducking stool was found, by a borough court against an adulteress.[2] Similarly, a pioneering study of the Devon quarter sessions between 1558 and 1714 found only one occasion on which that court ordered its use, in this instance against a scold, and even then only if the woman failed to mend her ways.[3] The records of manorial and borough courts would doubtless present a more complex pattern: David Underdown, for example, has claimed that the ducking stool was possibly originally an urban device, used against a variety of offenders, and that it became more widely diffused, and more exclusively used against scolds, from the middle of the sixteenth century.[4] Yet the ducking stool features most prominently in the local court records when jurors presented examples of the device as being disused or out of repair. This suggests that this celebrated form of punishment was, in fact, very rarely employed.[5]

There is rather more evidence for the use of the stocks, typically a wooden device which held the feet of offenders, thus immobilizing them and leaving them open to public display. But even here there are complications, as the stocks might also be used, in isolated villages, as a sort of holding prison in which offenders would be kept before being conveyed to the county gaol. When employed as a punishment, they seem to have been used most often against petty offenders, notably drunkards who were unable to pay the statutory 5s. fine for their offence, or petty thieves. The stocks were most used by the local courts, and do not figure much in the assize or quarter sessions records which have formed the basis for most research into crime and punishment. Analysis of the records of the Home Circuit of the assizes, for example, reveals only scattered use of the stocks between 1558 and 1625, those upon whom the punishment was inflicted including persons convicted for lodging vagrants or for less serious forms of witchcraft. Other evidence shows how the stocks could, on occasion, be used to give very full publicity to the offence being punished. Sometimes this might be done by attaching a paper naming the offence to the forehead or hat of the offender, while on occasion it might be done more symbolically, with, for example, weavers convicted for embezzling yarn being placed in the stocks with skeins of wool about their necks.[6]

The pillory, a device in which offenders stood with their head and hands between two pieces of wood, served much the same purpose: punishment involved placing the guilty party on display. The crowds attending such displays, however, seem to have been more likely to show their disapproval forcefully than those observing people being stocked or, indeed, those attending executions. Some of those placed in the pillory, notably such as were found guilty of homosexual offences or sex offences against children, were treated very roughly by those who gathered to witness their punishment, and there are a number of instances in which men standing on the pillory were killed. Despite such instances (most of which occurred around London) examination of provincial archives suggests that the pillory was infrequently used, and most often against fairly mundane offenders who were unlikely to attract very severe treatment from the mob. Thus surviving documentation shows that only about eighty people suffered on the pillory after trial on the Home Circuit of the assizes between 1558 and 1625, the bulk of them for non-capital witchcraft or seditious words. Yet here too the penalty could be adjusted and elaborated to meet individual circumstances. As with the stocks, the publicity value of the pillory might be enhanced by attaching a paper announcing the nature of the offence being punished. More rarely, punishment on the pillory might be accompanied by mutilation. Thus a Kent labourer convicted in 1599 for declaring that 'the Queen's Majestie was Antichrist and therefore she is throwne down into hell' was sentenced to be pilloried and to have his ears cut off, while a Colchester yeoman convicted in 1579 for calling the Earls of Warwick and Leicester traitors was sentenced to stand on the pillory in the town's market place and have his ear nailed to the pillory as he stood.[7] Such cases were, however, very rare.

Another form of public punishment, less familiar to the modern reader, was carting. This seems to have been most often used in urban areas, and was probably most frequently employed against brothel-keepers, prostitutes, and other offenders against sexual morality. The records of the quarter sessions of Middlesex, which already in Elizabeth I's reign encompassed a substantial built-up area on the fringes of London, contain a number of references to the practice. In 1576 a man described as being a person of evil life and reputation, a pimp, adulterer, fornicator and keeper of a common brothel house, was ordered to be driven in a cart from Newgate to St Giles's church on the next market day. In 1579 John Bellman of St John Street, Clerkenwell, Middlesex, was carted 'for that he hath lodged lewde persons in his house, and also . . . lewde wemenn delyverd of chylde in his house'. In 1591 one Atkynson and Jane the wife of William Isloppe were carted for committing adultery in Isloppe's house. Once more, we find evidence that the punishment could become more elaborate in appropriate cases, at times very much taking on the aspect of a skimmington or stang riding, those forms of community action to satirize or shame deviants. Thus a brothel-keeper named Elizabeth Hollande was put in a cart at Newgate and paraded around urban Middlesex with a paper naming her offence attached to her with people striking basins in front of her, whipped at Bridewell, and then placed in Newgate until she had paid a fine of £40 and given sureties for her good behaviour. One suspects that the impact of all this on Hollande was only slightly greater than it was on the neighbourhood.[8]

Although our emphasis in this section will be on the punishments awarded by the secular courts, it is worth remembering that in the early modern period England also possessed a system of ecclesiastical courts which were empowered to try a number of religious and moral offences. The most serious sanction which the ecclesiastical courts had at their disposal was excommunication, a form of religious ostracism which carried, in theory at least, serious religious and secular implications for those upon whom it was imposed. In practice, it is uncertain how much of a burden excommunication was regarded as by the bulk of the population. Certainly, the regular presentment of persons before the church courts for 'standing excommunicate' suggests that many people were able to cope with whatever disadvantages excommunication involved. The other main penalty imposed by the church courts was public penance, which again involved public punishment and shaming. The convicted person was to stand in church during the Sunday service, clad in a white sheet, carrying a white wand, sometimes having a paper announcing their offence attached to their head, sometimes making a public declaration of sorrow. As might be expected, it is uncertain how seriously penance was taken.

Puritan proponents of more serious penalties for those moral offences which penance so often punished argued that it was regarded as trivial by most people, although there is some contradictory evidence. Whatever the case, penance only made sense in a context where the church played an active role in social discipline, and where community values were regarded as crucial in that respect.[9]

Religion, in a rather different sense, also lay behind one of the more common penalties inflicted by the secular courts, the branding of convicted felons claiming benefit of clergy. The origins of this practice lay in disputes over the monarch's right to try criminous clergymen, dating from the high middles ages. It became accepted that clergymen convicted for felony should be handed over to the ecclesiastical authorities for punishment on a first offence, clerical status being established by the ability to read. A statute of 1489 regulated the existing system, making the reading test central, and declaring that on a first conviction offenders should be branded 'on the brawn of the left thumb' with M for murder or T for theft. The brand acted as proof of a first conviction: on the second the offender would be hanged. Statutory exceptions rapidly took a number of more serious felonies out of clergy, yet over the period 1550–1700 benefit of clergy was regularly in use, being most frequently extended to men found guilty of grand larceny or manslaughter. Even by 1489 it was obvious that few of those claiming clergy were clerics, and over the Elizabethan and Stuart periods this anomalous practice served as a major alternative to capital punishment.

Another punishment frequently inflicted by the assizes and quarter sessions was whipping. This penalty was most frequently employed against those found guilty of petty larceny (i.e. the theft of goods valued at less than a shilling) and vagrancy, although other offenders, notably unmarried mothers or other transgressors against sexual morality, might also suffer it. Whipping was normally carried out in public, with the offender either tied to a whipping post or to the end of a cart. The instrument used to inflict the punishment seems to have been some sort of cat-o'-nine-tails, and the punishment was obviously no light one. The number of strokes to be inflicted was rarely stated, but it was usually made clear that blood should be drawn, while the distances walked at the cart's end were often considerable.

Nevertheless, many thieves suffered whipping as a result of the undervaluing of stolen goods, a practice which offered another regular means of escaping the death penalty. It had been established in the fourteenth century that the theft of goods worth less than a shilling (by 1600 a day's wage for some skilled manual workers) was petty larceny, and that those convicted of it should not suffer death. The inflation of the sixteenth century had reduced whatever sense this distinction had, and, as we shall see in a later section, by the seventeenth century large numbers of thieves were escaping the gallows due to the deliberate undervaluing by the courts of the goods they had stolen. Some idea of the frequency with which the penalty was used for minor thefts can be gauged from the records of the Essex assizes and quarter sessions between 1620 and 1680. Of 182 persons convicted for stealing poultry whose punishment is known 60 were whipped, of 155 convicted of stealing clothes and household linen 133 were whipped, of 57 convicted for stealing food 46 were whipped. Whipping was thus evidently regarded as the major punishment for less serious forms of theft.[10]

Punishment in early modern England might hit the pocket as well as the body, for fining was long established as a penalty. Broadly, fines were used to punish two types of offence. Some offences, usually defined by statute, carried a set fine: thus Jacobean legislation made drunkards subject to a fine of 5s., while the more elaborate economic regulations created by Tudor legislation adjusted fines according to how long an illegal economic practice had been carried out. Otherwise, fines were very much at the discretion of the court, and might be adjusted to fit individual circumstances. Normally they were light. Assault, for example, was usually punished by fining, and analysis of assault charges tried at the Essex assizes and quarter sessions between 1620 and 1680 shows that in 81 of the 123 cases where the value of the fine inflicted is known the sum involved lay between one and 10s.[11] The records of local manorial courts, where fining was the usual penalty imposed, also show fines of a few pence or a few shillings being regularly inflicted on pilferers, scolds, and those presented for assault or bloodshed. Conversely, exceptional offenders or exceptional circumstances might prompt an exceptionally heavy fine. Thus when Thomas Cudmore, an Essex gentleman and grand juror, was fined an exemplary £500 for barratry in 1679, the relevant order attributed this penalty to 'the heynousness of his offence'.[12]

The great pillar of current penal practice, custodial punishment in a prison, was only very rarely employed before the eighteenth century. Fundamentally, as far as criminals were concerned, the prison was essentially the place where they would be held before trial, rather than a means of punishment. Given the state of most prisons in the sixteenth and seventeenth centuries, this was probably no bad thing. The records of any county's quarter sessions for that period provide ample evidence of ruinous gaols, numerous deaths from gaol fever, and brutal or negligent keepers: a neat illustration of the state of the gaols in the period comes from Warwickshire, where at one point in the 1620s the gaoler reported to the bench that the county gaol was so dilapidated that he was forced to keep the prisoners in his own house.[13] Even so, leaving debtors and the occasional political prisoner aside, there is some evidence that prison was beginning to be seen as a means of punishment in its modern sense. The witchcraft statute of 1563 enacted that persons convicted of less serious forms of witchcraft should be kept in prison for a year, during which time they would be pilloried on four occasions. In 1576 judges were given the option of imprisoning for a year persons to whom benefit of clergy had been granted. There were, moreover, isolated instances in which a term of imprisonment, often joined with other punishments, might be inflicted on convicted offenders.

Indeed, from the middle of the sixteenth century another institution, the house of correction, was gradually assuming many of the functions of the modern prison. The prototype house of correction was the London Bridewell, set up in the 1550s in the face of growing problems of vagrancy and poverty in the capital. Considerable local experimentation followed, but by the early seventeenth century most counties were served by a number of houses of correction, these institutions performing the functions of workhouses, hospitals and prisons. These early houses of correction, long familiar to historians of local administration in a general sort of way, are in urgent need of detailed investigation. What is obvious at present, however, is that they were being used, probably almost from their inception, as prisons for petty offenders. Most of their inmates were either vagrants or members of the disorderly local poor. To these were added a number of offenders for whom a spell in the house of correction was prescribed by statute, notably unmarried mothers, who were thought worthy of a year in the house of correction. The house also contained a spectrum of other offenders, most of them sent there, either by a court or upon summary conviction before justices of the peace, for a short spell: petty thieves, runaway apprentices, disorderly servants, poachers. Justices' notebooks from the seventeenth century suggest that the house of correction was considered by officials and the public alike as a handy means of dealing with such offenders, while some idea of attitudes can be gauged from the occasional practice, dating from around 1600, of sending persons acquitted of property offences at the assizes to the house of correction. Being found innocent of a specific offence did not, seemingly, imply that the accused led a blameless life. The house of correction was significant for two other reasons. Firstly, it has been claimed that the labour discipline envisaged in the houses' policy of putting offenders to work implies that the house of correction was a form of punishment connected to early capitalism. Secondly, the rationale behind the house of correction, the notion that those passing through it might possibly be amended by the process, could be portrayed as prefiguring later ideas on reforming through punishment. Unfortunately, too little is known about conditions in the early houses of correction to comment fully on either of these hypotheses. Yet it remains clear that the setting up of a system of houses of correction in every county was one of the major, and most novel, developments in the field of punishment over the seventeenth century.[14]

As this brief sketch has demonstrated, early modern England possessed a wide variety of punishments which had a distinctive rationale and which offered a potentially flexible response to the need to punish criminals. The broader intention behind these punishments was overwhelmingly deterrent and retributive: the insistence on the public nature of punishment, which would both encourage the community to believe that wickedness was receiving its just deserts, and deter potential offenders, is sufficient demonstration of this point. It is, moreover, as we have hinted, possible to see some uncertain signs of reformatory notions in the house of correction. Yet our review of early modern punishment has so far virtually ignored the penalty that was not only the most serious, but which also, arguably, characterized the penal thinking of the period: death. The death penalty took a variety of forms in early modern England. Peers of the realm were entitled to be beheaded, this being thought of as less degrading than other forms of execution. Felons caught in Halifax, apparently unique in having its own local method of inflicting death, might be punished by a form of primitive guillotine. Persons convicted of treason, a category of offender which included wives who had murdered their husbands and servants who had murdered their employers, suffered aggravated forms of death. Male traitors were subjected to the barbarities of hanging, drawing and quartering, while women were burnt at the stake. But the most common form of capital punishment, to which literally thousands of convicted felons were subjected, was hanging. It is, accordingly, to this institution that we shall turn in the next section.

The Rise and Fall of Capital Punishment

The Tudor period was one which saw a marked harshening of the criminal code. This was a complex process, but at its basis lay that tightening of governmental style which has led some historians to talk of a 'Tudor Revolution in Government', and which, however unhappy other historians may be with this term, manifested itself in a variety of ways. Intertwined with this were the implications of the Reformation. The Tudor law of treason was obviously made more complicated by this event, while the heightened sensibilities about human propensities to wickedness inherent in protestant theology made the godly rulers of protestant England very sensitive to law and order issues. The sixteenth century thus witnessed a proliferation of laws either creating new offences, or redefining old ones, the end product in either case being to create a series of felonies outside benefit of clergy. A statute of 1532 set the tone for the remainder of the century by stipulating that those committing petty treason, wilful murder, highway robbery, or who stole from churches or other holy places or from dwelling houses where the owner or members of the household were present, and who burned down houses or barns where grain was stored were, with the exception of high ranking clergymen, to be denied benefit of clergy. Later acts extended the principle to: those holding 'diversity of opinion' over religion (1540); those indulging in witchcraft or sorcery (1542); servants stealing or embezzling goods worth more than 40 shillings from their masters (1536); horse thieves (1546); and those committing buggery with mankind or animals (1532). The short reigns of Edward VI (1547–53) and Mary Tudor (1553–8) confused the issue, but after the accession of Elizabeth I yet more capital offences entered the statute book, and a number of Henry VIII's statutes which had been repealed were virtually re-enacted.

This intensification of the law against felony followed two centuries where there had been little new legislation creating capital crime, and during which, as far as we can tell, actual levels of capital punishment were fairly low. Isolated samples of court materials suggest that the incidence of hanging was sometimes very low indeed. Thus the Warwickshire justices of the peace indicted 231 people for felony between 1377 and 1397. The fate of 169 of these can be discerned: of this total, 86 were outlawed, 44 acquitted, and a mere 13 hanged. A fuller sample analysed by Barbara Hanawalt, consisting of 15,865 persons accused of felony before the assizes of 8 counties between 1300 and 1348, suggests a low conviction rate, especially for rape and homicide. Interestingly, Hanawalt suggests that this low conviction rate was the outcome of a feeling that the main available punishment, hanging, was considered too serious for the offences involved. If this interpretation is correct, it would appear that even in the fourteenth century a higher conviction rate may have been obtained had proper secondary punishments been available.[15]

The crucial problem is the extent to which the harshness of the legal code which seems to have set in during the second half of Henry VIII's reign was matched by an increased severity on the part of the courts. Unfortunately, the assize records upon which any answer to this question would have to be based are largely missing for the early sixteenth century. Two north-western counties,

Lancashire and Cheshire, enjoyed palatinate jurisdictions, which kept them outside the assize system, and the records of their criminal courts are largely intact. These archives are difficult to use for the period in question, and so far have attracted little scholarly attention. Early soundings in the Lancashire records, however, suggest that a high proportion of those accused of felony, in some sessions maybe half of them, suffered capital punishment in the 1540s.[16] There is also the intriguing tradition that 70,000 'rogues' were executed during the reign of Henry VIII (1509–47). This figure is obviously a gross exaggeration, but it might well represent some folk-memory of what had been a real increase in judicial severity against convicted felons. Certainly such an increase, given what we have said about the legislative harshness of Henry VIII's reign, would have made sense: the toughening of official attitudes which more stringent laws indicated ought logically to have been accompanied by harsher attitudes in the courts.

Certainly, when archive survival makes it possible to pick up the story in more detail later in the sixteenth century, there is every indication that sentencing policy was harsh. Examination of the fate of 10,107 male felons (female felons were, broadly speaking, ineligible for the main secondary punishment, branding after the granting of benefit of clergy, and are therefore less relevant for our immediate purposes) for whom details of crime and punishment survive for the Home Circuit of the assizes (comprising the counties of Essex, Hertfordshire, Kent, Surrey and Sussex) over the period 1560–1625 shows a decline in the incidence of death sentences. Of those accused of felony, 27.4 per cent were sentenced to death in the decade 1560–9, and 28.2 per cent in 1570–9. Similarly the Middlesex Sessions witnessed very high levels of capital convictions over the mid sixteenth century, 41 per cent of those accused of felony in the 1550s, 52 per cent in the 1570s. In both jurisdictions percentages of those capitally convicted had fallen drastically by the early 1620s, to 17.2 per cent and 14.5 per cent respectively. Statistics derived from the Court of Great Sessions of Cheshire, a palatinate jurisdiction enjoying the best survival of relevant documentation from the period, permits us to trace longer term trends. A high proportion of felons tried before that court (over 20 per cent in the 1580s and 1620s) were capitally convicted in the late sixteenth and early seventeenth centuries, a much lower proportion (around 10 per cent) in the late seventeenth and early eighteenth. This fall in the proportion of accused being capitally convicted was paralleled by a fall in absolute totals. An estimated 111 felons were sentenced to death in Cheshire in the 1590s, 166 in the 1620s, but only 10 in the first decade of the eighteenth century. Fragmentary evidence from other areas (notably the Home Counties and Devon) suggests that neither of these trends was unique to Cheshire. Even in London, with its massive and increasing population and its allegedly unique law and order problems, there is every suggestion that executions in the early eighteenth century were at a far lower level of frequency than they had been in the reign of James I a century previously.[17]

This is all very puzzling, given what both the pattern of legislative activity and received wisdom about the broad lines of socio-economic change would suggest. As is well known, after 1688 the English parliament passed a long series of laws which, by 1800, had placed some 200 capital offences, many of them property crimes, on the statute book. This 'Bloody Code', directed as it was largely against property offences, has been thought of as symbolizing England's transition towards becoming a more commercial and more bourgeois society. Following on from this argument, it is undeniable that everything we know about England's economic development over the late seventeenth and eighteenth centuries suggests that, logically, property offences should have been increasing in number and that those committing them should have been treated more severely by the courts. Beneath all this lurks the general contention that the period *c.* 1500–1800 witnessed the transition from a 'feudal' criminality based on violence to a 'capitalist' one based on property offences. Over a very long run, such a transition undoubtedly took place: but there is little indication of its presence in sixteenth- and seventeenth-century England.

Indeed, such archival evidence as has been analysed suggests that England, the London area probably excepted, experienced a massive drop in indicted crimes against property between 1590 and 1750, a shift which was accompanied by a corresponding drop in capital convictions for such offences. Analysis of felonies tried at the Court of Great Sessions at Chester, to take a well documented example, demonstrates the following pattern:

Period	Total death sentences	For property offences	For homicide	For other felonies
1580–1619	337	294 (87.0%)	35 (10.5%)	8 (2.5%)
1620–1659	274	210 (76.5)%	49 (18.0%)	15 (5.5%)
1660–1669	85	47 (55.5%)	31 (36.5%)	7 (8.0%)

The records for Essex, a more economically advanced county than Cheshire which also enjoys reasonable documentation, show a less marked but essentially similar pattern, especially if allowance is made for the relatively poor survival of the Essex records before 1650. Thus such statistics for capital punishment as have so far been derived from Elizabethan and seventeenth-century court archives raise the paradoxical suggestion that, if harsh treatment of property offenders is a hallmark of the arrival of a bourgeois or commercial ethic among ruling groups, this ethic was considerably stronger in 1600 than it was in the early eighteenth century.[18]

Other surprises occur when we attempt to uncover the history of the rituals which surrounded executions. Hanging was a public event, and it has long been known that large crowds attended executions. Most of our images of such events are derived from eighteenth-century accounts, particularly those of metropolitan executions at Tyburn. This eighteenth-century evidence has usually been adduced by historians to demonstrate the brutality of the period. More sensitive treatment has been afforded to the public execution more recently, and the conclusion that the Tyburn rituals had a deep importance in representing a point of contact between popular and élite culture is intriguing.[19] Yet even here, the focus has been exclusively on the eighteenth century. Examination of the issue over a longer timespan, however, suggests that the decisive changes in the rituals surrounding public execution, along with the first wave of legislative harshness and the rise in the number of capital convictions, occurred around the middle of the sixteenth century. There is little evidence that any elaborate ceremonial attended the execution of felons in the later middle ages, or that they were expected to indulge in that central component of later public executions, the gallows speech. Both the ceremonial and the set-piece speech seem to have been sixteenth-century innovations, owing much to the need for greater ideological control to which the

Tudor state felt obliged to aspire in the decades following the Reformation. The change first becomes apparent in the well-documented trials and executions of traitors. In a spirit comparable to the show trials of Stalin's Russia, convicted traitors characteristically used their last speech not as an occasion for hurling abuse or defiance at the regime sending them to their death, but rather as a means of emphasizing their guilt, of expressing their sorrow for their transgressions, for wishing the monarch under whose laws they suffered a long and glorious reign, and for reminding their listeners (and those who read the later printed accounts of their speeches) of the virtues of obedience to the law, the monarch, and the will of God. By the late sixteenth century these sentiments were also being voiced by low-born felons.[20]

The growth and elaboration of the ceremonies and rituals which surrounded public execution were, I would contend, as important and as indicative of change as were the numerous statutes broadening the scope of offences for which the death penalty could be imposed and the grim statistics showing how frequently hanging occurred. At a time when the coming together of large crowds of common people was not encouraged, the authorities allowed thousands to gather at public executions. These were no mere displays of brutality, but were complex phenomena acquiring a complex ceremonial. The convicted person might be taken to the gallows in a procession, and once there, as we have suggested, would be allowed to make an elaborate speech. By 1618 the clergyman Henry Goodcole was to accept it as axiomatic that

> dying men's wordes are ever remarkable, & their last deeds memorable for succeeding posterities, by them to be instructed, what vertues or vices they followed and imbraced, and by them to learne to imitate that which was good, and eschew evill. . .[21]

What is important for our immediate purposes is that the publicity afforded to these 'dying men's wordes' as recorded in the gallows speeches seems to have become an especially urgent issue for the post-Reformation state. Through these 'last dying speeches', as well as through the ritual surrounding public execution from which they arose, execution became not just a simple demonstration that crime did not pay, but rather a more sophisticated underpinning of that ideological control to which contemporary regimes aspired. This control was made all the more desirable by the awareness that every early modern regime possessed of the limitations of its capacity for physical control.[22]

An important element in the elaboration of the execution ritual, and in the construction of a stereotyped pattern of behaviour on the gallows, and of a stereotyped last dying speech, was the involvement of the clergy. Many of the accounts of executions which have survived were written by clergymen, and even those which were not make it clear that members of the clergy were active in 'working on' the person awaiting death. Their major purposes in so doing were to ensure that the offender left the world in a proper religious state, that they were reconciled to their fate, and that they were, in a certain sense, morally reintegrated into the society whose laws they had broken. One of the most striking of these clerical interventions is recorded in the early life of that hero of English protestantism, William Perkins. Between 1581 and 1584 Perkins acted as chaplain to the prisoners in Cambridge gaol. During that time Perkins apparently came across a young felon who was already on the gallows, and who was apparently none too happy about his fate. Perkins 'laboured to cheer up his spirits', but, finding the task difficult, asked the lad if he was afraid of death. The felon replied that he was not afraid of death, 'but of a worser thing', by which he presumably meant eternal damnation. Perkins called him down from the gallows, promising to show him 'what God's grace will do to strengthen thee'. The account of the incident continues,

> Whereupon the prisoner coming down, master Perkins took him by the hand, and made him kneel down with himself at the ladder's foot . . . when that blessed man of God made such an effectual prayer in confession of sins . . . as made the prisoner burst into abundance of tears: and Master Perkins, finding that he had brought him low enough, even to hell gates, he proceeded to the second part of his prayer, and therein to show him the Lord Jesus . . . stretching forth his blessed hand for mercy . . . which he did so sweetly press with such heavenly art . . . as made him break into new showers of tears of joy of the inward consolation which he found . . . who (the prayer being ended) rose from his knees cheerfully, and went up the ladder again so comforted, and took his death with such patience and

alacrity, as if he actually saw himself delivered from the hell which he feared before, and heaven opened for the receiving of his soul.[23]

I would contend that such clerical preoccupations and successes were characteristic of public executions in the late sixteenth and seventeenth centuries. On the strength of the existing state of research, there seems to have been little of this active clerical involvement in the later middle ages, while, despite the best efforts and frequent successes of many clergymen, the religious input seems to have been less marked in the eighteenth.

It is largely this religious dimension, as well as the suspicion that the public execution was a more significant phenomenon than might at first appear, that makes it difficult to write the whole process off as something which simply symbolized the brutality of past ages. It is difficult to divest ourselves of the carnivalesque, gin-sodden, Hogarthian mobs which are so much a part of the image which has been created of eighteenth-century Tyburn. Wider evidence suggests that the crowds at executions were, on occasion, orderly and moved by the spectacle before them. Some accounts, indeed, express surprise when the offender on the gallows failed to perform the allotted role. Thus the Yorkshire nonconformist Ralph Thoresby was surprised when, in 1682, he witnessed the execution of a murderer who refused to acknowledge his guilt on the scaffold, and died unrepentant. Thoresby noted that this attitude not only 'struck tears into my heart', but also left the 'many thousand spectators' who had gathered 'exceedingly frustrated in their expectations'.[24] Again and again, this sort of sentiment is to be found in accounts of public executions: the idea that the convicted person ought to die accepting his or her fate, and confessing their crimes and the lesser sins which had prefaced them. These were doubtless the 'expectations' of the crowd whose disappointment Thoresby recorded in 1682, which suggests that they were very different from the animalistic mob of popular history. Very frequently, indeed, we are confronted by accounts which stress the crowd's compassion for the person on the gallows, as long as they played their role correctly. Thus when Joan Cason was hanged after a tragically bungled trial for witchcraft in 1586, we are told that she made so godly and penitent an end that many now lamented her death that were before her utter enemies. Yea, some now wished her alive after she was hanged, that cried for the hangman when she was alive . . .[25]

We should not take too cosy a view of public execution; yet it is obvious that the whole business, and the reactions of the crowds present, were much more complex than might at first appear.

By the late seventeenth century, therefore, levels of execution were lower, in both absolute terms and relevant to the number of persons accused of capital offences, than they had been a century previously, and were also surrounded by a theatre of punishment in which most actors knew, and generally played, their part. The problem remains of accounting for the massive decline in levels of execution in the middle of the seventeenth century. At the moment, any suggestions raised over this matter must be regarded as very tentative: even so, a number of possible ways into the explanation of this remarkable shift can already be suggested. Firstly, turning to the wider events of the mid seventeenth century, we find that the aftermath of the Civil War brought demands for law reform, one of the most persistent of which being for the limitation of the use of the death penalty, particularly for property offences.[26] It is possible that the airing of this widespread disquiet about capital punishment may have been one Interregnum development which survived the post-Restoration reaction.

Related to this is the need to study judicial attitudes. Some scholars[27] have suggested that a 'judicial revolution' occurred over the sixteenth and seventeenth centuries. Certainly it now seems that there was a growing professionalism among English legal practitioners over the early seventeenth century, and this may have led to changing attitudes, and a greater degree of competence.[28] It has also been argued that the broader intellectual changes of the seventeenth century encouraged a stricter attitude to the laws of evidence in the legal mind.[29] It is uncertain how all this would necessarily lead to lower levels of execution, but it is clear that the attitudes of the judiciary towards punishment is an area where further investigation might well prove instructive.

It is also worthwhile to speculate how far continental comparisons might help illuminate the English situation. There are obvious difficulties here: different legal codes and different court systems make comparisons unusually dangerous. Yet it is encouraging to discover that one of the fullest accounts of developments in another European context over the period in question, that of Richard van Dülmen (1986) paints a picture which is, both qualitatively and quantitatively, similar to that which we have delineated for Tudor and Stuart England. This study, based on German city archives, shows the development of scaffold rituals after about 1500, the heavy injection of religion into the ceremonial of punishment over the sixteenth century, and a growing importance of secular elements during the eighteenth. There was also a massive decline in absolute levels of execution over the first half of the seventeenth century, with levels generally staying low in the late seventeenth and eighteenth centuries. This suggests that England's experience was not a unique one. In particular, the mid seventeeth-century fall in capital convictions in England is probably best interpreted as one aspect of that general European transition in which society moved away from feeling itself to be constantly under pressure and in danger of disintegration towards being able to take a more measured and self-confident view of things. Beneath this transition, there lay much deeper socio-economic and demographic changes.

The Search for Secondary Punishments

To most general historians, as we have implied, judicial punishment in the eighteenth century has been epitomized by public execution, and, in particular, public execution at Tyburn. Literary and visual images, the remarks of foreign tourists, knowledge of the Bloody Code: all of these have combined to persuade later writers that the eighteenth century witnessed the apex of the death penalty's development. In fact, the actual levels of execution were lower than they had been in the decades around 1600, while the ceremonials so frequently referred to in accounts of Tyburn executions were hardly new. The actual statistics of capital punishment provide a rather more complex impression over the eighteenth century than general histories would suggest. Figures for London and Middlesex show that there was over the eighteenth century as a whole a growing gap between the number of persons capitally convicted and those actually executed: between 1756 and 1765, for example, 329 persons were capitally convicted, but only 183 executed, figures which changed respectively to 819 and 132 between 1795 and 1804. Obviously, despite the increasing severity of the legal code, the number of those suffering the death penalty was falling, especially in relation to population, while those being executed were obviously being selected from a wider group. However, the numbers of those executed could fluctuate: 101 persons were executed in London and Middlesex in 1785, and 92 in 1787, but a mere 6 suffered in 1759, and 7 in 1794.[30]

More recently John Beattie's researches, concentrated mainly on Surrey, have added greatly to our understanding of developments in capital punishment over the eighteenth century, and have helped to clarify some of the problems inherent in the statistics for London and Middlesex. About 7 persons were hanged annually in Surrey in 1660, the date at which Beattie's study commences. By about 1800, despite the fact that the population of the county had more than doubled, only about 6 persons a year (or about 30 per cent of those capitally convicted) were executed. There had been various peaks and troughs in levels of execution in the intervening period (notably a level of about 13 executions a year in the 1730s). Surviving documentation shows that 481 men and 37 women were hanged between 1663 and 1802. Of this total, 84 per cent suffered for property offences, and 9 per cent for murder or infanticide. Beattie's researches thus reinforce the contention that property offences were those most likely to be punished by death in the eighteenth century. But they also demonstrate that levels of execution did not show a uniform trend over the century. They tended to fluctuate, and the percentage of those actually executed over the eighteenth century, even in periods of severity like the 1720s or the years around 1780, was always much lower, and usually less than half, of those capitally convicted.[31]

This last point leads us into the problem of how contemporaries saw the legal code as operating. As we have suggested, most people before the eighteenth century (a few Interregnum radicals apart) probably thought of the criminal law as being so much of a part of things that the need to justify it was otiose. The eighteenth century, however, did see a developing debate over crime and punishment, in which discussion of capital punishment was a recurring theme. Indeed, the century virtually opened with a remarkable pamphlet entitled 'Hanging not Punishment Enough for Murtherers, Highway Men, and House Breakers, etc'.[32] This, as its title suggests, recommended nastier forms of execution for serious offenders, since larceny, clearly a less serious crime, could be punished by hanging. More mainstream attitudes, however, were demonstrated later in the century when the Bloody Code began to attract adverse comment. Its defenders, notably the Reverend William Paley, adopted what seemed to them a perfectly logical line. Obviously, a penal code as draconian as England's could and should not be applied in its full severity upon every offender: it was important, however, to have on the statute book laws which would make it possible to punish offenders as severely as possible when it was felt appropriate to do so. As Paley put it, it was essential to retain the power to impose the death penalty for 'every crime which under any possible circumstances, may merit the punishment of death', in the full knowledge that in practice execution should be reserved for 'a small proportion of each class . . . the general character, or peculiar aggravation of whose crimes, render them fit examples of public justice'. The key to understanding the operation of the criminal law in the eighteenth, and indeed earlier, centuries lies in grasping the fundamental fact that it was applied selectively.[33]

The importance of this point was vividly signposted in an essay published in 1975 by Douglas Hay which, whatever the criticisms levelled against it,[34] is still essential reading for anybody attempting to understand the rationale of capital punishment in the eighteenth century. The most relevant part of Hay's argument for our immediate purposes is the stress he placed on mercy. To Hay, eighteenth-century criminal law was basically an instrument by which the privileged defended their property, and thus constructed the Bloody Code as a barrier against property offenders. It was soon realized, however, that if every property offender at risk of being executed were actually to be hanged, disquiet would have been caused by the sheer numbers of bodies festooning the gallows at the end of every assize. Judges, therefore, made full use of the prerogative of mercy: those offenders who were hanged performed a deterrent role, while those who were pardoned or suffered lesser punishments felt grateful and congratulated themselves on living under the laws of England. Thus selectivity in the application of capital punishment preserved the hegemony of the ruling classes more effectively than simple repression would have done, all the more so in that the pardoning process, by bringing in locally powerful people as character witnesses for the accused, helped flatter gentry notions as to the importance of their role as patron. Arguably, none of this was altogether new: fragmentary materials suggest that such practices were already firmly entrenched by the late sixteenth century.[35] But they were much more widely practised in the eighteenth, and are certainly better documented.

The factors affecting whether there would be a high or a low level of executions at any one assize or in any one year, or whether any particular felon should suffer hanging, were varied. One of Hay's critics, Peter King, has explored the criteria upon which the decision to execute might be based. These are roughly what might have been expected. On his sample, taken from Essex sources between 1787 and 1790, those escaping death tended to have a previous good character, to be young, to have no previous convictions, to be able to provide a character reference from a previous master or employer, and capable of arguing convincingly that they had been coerced into crime by others. Those executed tended to have a previous bad character and/or previous convictions, to have committed a crime which was felt to be inherently wicked or against which, it was currently felt, examples had to be made, to be part of a dangerous gang, and to be young men in their twenties with no familial or established employment connections. The worst time to commit a crime was when the authorities were worried by what they thought of as rising levels of crime or a more general social dislocation. In particular, the period immediately after a war normally witnessed high levels of execution: the return from the army and navy of large numbers of males from the labouring poor created both a higher level of crime and a panic on the part of the authorities which led to a higher level of executions.[36]

Selectivity, then, lay at the heart of eighteenth-century punishment: the problem remained, however, of working out what to do with those convicted criminals who were not selected to hang. The eighteenth century has most often been thought of, as far as the history of punishment is concerned, as the era of the death penalty: yet what is really remarkable about the century's penal policy is the almost constant search for viable secondary punishments.[37] There had, of course, long been other ways of treating offenders than hanging them. The right to pardon probably went back as far as the right to punish, and sixteenth-century archives regularly show examples of pardoning in action. Isolated felons or traitors would escape through being well connected, or through being able to make convincing cases to judges or the central authorities. More rarely, whole groups of offenders might find themselves pardoned due to some happy accident: the accession of a new monarch, for example, normally meant that less serious felons would be pardoned. But such practices, although useful enough as occasional symbols, were unlikely to form the basis for changes in regular sentencing.

At the beginning of the period with which this book is concerned, 1550, convicted felons might escape the noose by successfully pleading benefit of clergy. The basic criterion for so doing was the ability to read, an ability which was almost non-existent among the lower orders, the group most likely to commit most crimes, in the sixteenth century. That benefit of clergy was frequently claimed, therefore, suggests that judges were using it flexibly as a means of providing an escape route for convicted felons. Certainly, there is scattered evidence that the reading test was not being very rigorously applied. The tradition that the passage to be read to prove literacy should be the opening verse of the 51st Psalm gave felons the chance to learn the relevant lines by rote, although there are examples of judges directing prisoners to read other parts of the Bible in cases where they wished to be severe. More frequently, perhaps, judges were willing to accept very poor efforts at reading. Sir Thomas Smith, writing in the mid sixteenth century, thought that many of those claiming clergy read 'God knoweth sometime very slenderly'. In 1655 it was claimed that 'were it not for the favour of the court, not one in twenty could save their lives by reading', while in 1589 another problem had been identified when an Essex JP wrote to Lord Burghley that 'under pretence or pity, or favouring of life (as they call it)' Home Circuit judges were allowing clergy to convicted felons who had already been branded. The old procedures were effectively bypassed by a statute of 1705, which made clergy automatically available to all first offenders in cases where it might normally have been granted. But it is obvious that long before that date judges were using awards of benefit of clergy on dubious grounds as a means of mitigating the severity of the criminal code.[38]

Indeed, statistics derived from court archives point to the growing use of this practice over the second half of the seventeenth century. At the Essex assizes, the proportion of convicted male felons claiming their clergy successfully rose from about a third in the period 1566–70 to over half in the 1580s. At the Court of Great Sessions in Cheshire, the percentage rose from 14.75 in 1566–70 to a peak of 38.7 in 1591–5. Clergy continued to be a regular aspect of sentencing over the seventeenth century: in Essex, for example, 524 thieves (or 47 per cent of those suffering physical punishment) convicted at the assizes and quarter sessions between 1620 and 1680 claimed benefit of clergy. Such figures suggest that the reading test was a nonsense: over the seventeenth century as a whole, it is doubtful if more than 5 per cent of the labouring poor could read. Benefit of clergy was essentially a method by which the court might adopt a more flexible attitude to punishment, while cases late in the sixteenth century where clergy was granted after confession probably furnish early examples of plea-bargaining.[39]

The extension of benefit of clergy to women obviously presented a few logical problems, although a statute of 1624 did so in cases of thefts of small value. Women, however, had their own means of escaping hanging. Under English law, a pregnant woman could not be hanged: the innocent embryo should not suffer for the mother's crime. Accordingly, the law held that a pregnant woman under sentence of death should be delivered of her child, and then executed subsequently. In practice, it appears that the implementation of the death penalty in such circumstances was a very uncertain process. J. S. Cockburn's research into the records of the Home Circuit has revealed just how frequently this 'benefit of the belly' was claimed. On the strength of surviving documentation, 1,624 women were accused of felony on the Home Circuit between 1559 and 1625. Of these 711 (44 per cent) were convicted, of whom 267 (38 per cent) were found to be pregnant, and 257 (36 per cent) sentenced to death. Even in a period of demographic expansion, it seems unlikely that over a third of women convicted of felony should be pregnant, and it is probable that the 'juries of matrons' who searched them to establish pregnancy frequently stretched the evidence in their favour, as did judges. To Cockburn, the plea of pregnancy was in many ways 'a judicially controlled fiction', which was 'manipulated to give assize judges considerable discretion in the punishment of female felons'. As with the decision to award benefit of clergy, the accused's age, reputation, behaviour in court, and the gravity of the crime in question all contributed to the accepting of a plea of pregnancy.[40]

Although it is more difficult to quantify, lowering the value of goods stolen in larceny cases to below a shilling was also common throughout the late sixteenth and seventeenth centuries. This was usually done in one of two ways, both of them involving the connivance of the accuser, the jury, the judge, and the clerical staff of the court involved. Firstly, stolen goods would be listed on the relevant indictment at a ridiculously low price: a stolen pig might be valued at 10d. on the indictment, for example, when supporting depositions revealed that it had been sold for three or four shillings. Secondly, the trial jury (perhaps under the direction of the judge) would either find that the stolen item in question was worth less than a shilling, or select an appropriately priced item from a list of stolen goods, and find the accused guilty for that alone. The comments of contemporaries[41] suggest that the decision to opt for leniency would depend upon such factors as the nature of the offender, the circumstances of the time at which the offence was committed, and the seriousness with which the offence was viewed. Once more, we find ourselves confronting the great principle of selectivity.

Whipping, the plea of pregnancy, and benefit of clergy were all long established in 1650. From about that date, however, the courts began to adopt what was to be one of the main forms of judicial punishment for the next two centuries: the transportation of convicted felons to English, and later British, colonies. The practice, philosophically speaking, had its origins in the ancient punishment of banishment, something which had fallen into disuse in England with the arrival of the Tudor dynasty. More immediately, transportation seems to have been envisaged occasionally in the late

Elizabethan and early Stuart periods, although there is little doubt that it was first established as a means of dealing with felons on a regular basis in the years following Charles II's Restoration in 1660. There was probably a feeling of dissatisfaction with benefit of clergy, and an awareness of the need to find some sort of middle course between hanging felons and sending them back into society with a branded left hand. By 1663 transportation of convicted felons to the West Indies or North America as a condition of pardon was seen as a measure likely to be advantageous to offender and society alike. A royal warrant of that year declared that such a policy would 'become our royal clemency and be likewise an advantage to the public', while in the same year we find convicted felons petitioning for transportation as a condition for pardon on the grounds that they were 'unmarried and all able to do good service and steadfastly resolving through God's assistance to amend their lives for the future'.[42] Thus a few offenders made the trip westwards in the later seventeenth century, most of them bound to perform seven years' service.

By the 1680s, however, transportation was running into difficulties. Black slaves were regarded as a better investment by planters and more profitable by the merchants who normally contracted to take the convicts over, while a number of colonies passed laws prohibiting the landing of convicts on their shores. The desperation caused in official circles by the crime wave which followed the demobilization of the armed forces after the Treaty of Utrecht (1713) revived interest in the policy, however, and in 1718 a Transportation Act was passed. This made it possible for a non capital felon to be sentenced to transportation for seven years, and capital felons for fourteen years, returning to England before the expiration of these periods being a capital offence. The Act represented what was, by the standards of the time, a formidable investment of governmental energy and the taxpayers' money in a penal policy. The Act envisaged central government co-ordination and support for the scheme and, in the London area at least, contracts with merchants shipping convicts out were arranged by the Treasury. Between 1718 and the end of transportation to America in 1775, some 30,000 convicts were sent over from England, along with perhaps 13,000 from Ireland and 700 from

Scotland, most of them going to Virginia and Maryland.[43] The major consequence of this process for the English courts was that by the beginning of the 1720s benefit of clergy virtually disappeared as a form of punishment.[44] Whatever its advantages or disadvantages for the colonies, transportation to America rapidly established itself as a crucial element in the English system of judicial punishment.

The early eighteenth century also experienced a stirring of interest in imprisonment as means of punishment, rather than as a place where prisoners were held pending trial. As we have noted, the seventeenth-century gaol, on the strength of scattered evidence to be found in the assize and quarter sessions records of various counties, was frequently a decrepit and unhealthy place. By the early eighteenth century, however, there are indications that at least some county administrations were taking a more active interest in the state of the local prison's fabric and the health and welfare of prisoners: the neo-baroque York Castle county gaol, built in 1705, is an early piece of evidence for this trend. Some commentators were also interested in continental developments: the Maison de Force at Ghent; the Rome house of correction, with its inscription, 'It is little advantage to restrain the bad by punishment, unless you render them good by discipline'; even, a little later, prisons in Japan and China. Popular historians of the prison have, perhaps, overestimated the importance of John Howard, whose researches into prison conditions were to turn public opinion in favour of prison reform in the last quarter of the eighteenth century. Howard's energy and genius are undeniable: yet his writings had all the more impact because new ideas about the role of prisons were already present. As early as 1753, for example, Henry Fielding and the architect Thomas Gibson were projecting a huge house of correction with accommodation for 3,000 male paupers, 2,000 female paupers, and 1,000 convicts.[45]

Most innovations were considerably less grandiose than this scheme. As we have hinted, the most important input into the new use of the prison was a local and piecemeal process: certainly, there seems to have been no central direction, and no major reformer. Imprisonment was being considered as a suitable punishment for property offenders as early as the 1730s. By the middle of the eighteenth century, a few observers were also applauding the reformative virtues of hard labour: Joseph Massie, writing in 1758, could argue that if petty offenders were caught at an early stage and held in the house of correction 'to beat hemp or do other hard work' for a month or so they might well be fitted to return to an 'honest course of life'. In 1751 Joshua Fitzsimmonds had argued that, 'such punishments as branding, whipping and even transportation, might be very properly changed to hard labour and correction suitable to the nature of the crime.'[46] The idea that imprisonment, or a spell in the house of correction, combined with hard labour, might well be a useful means of dealing with the petty offender, was clearly gaining hold. In 1770 a committee of the House of Commons was set up to consider some of the elements of the criminal law relating to capital offences. This committee suggested that there should be a greater proportionality in the treatment of offences, and in particular that a less severe code would lead to more offenders being convicted, and also suggested that one of the objectives of punishment should be reformation. The Bill arising from this committee's deliberations was lost in 1772, but it is significant that from about that date imprisonment seems to have been used more regularly by the quarter sessions and assizes, although the impact of the end of transportation after the outbreak of the revolt of the American colonies in 1776 was obviously a key factor here.

Despite these early stirrings of an awareness of the potential of imprisonment as a form of punishment, it took more than a generation for disquiet at the Bloody Code to bear fruit in the form of full-scale attacks on capital punishment. By the 1780s parliamentary debates demonstrated a growing reluctance to pass new capital statutes, and by 1789 an MP could be found commenting on 'the proper aversion of the House, to the extension and increase of the penal statutes. Their number, undoubtedly, was already too great.'[47] The impact of the French Revolution then impeded any attempts at reform for more than two decades as the English *ancien régime* looked nervously across the Channel, and concluded that change in the criminal law (and, indeed, in almost anything else) might be the first step on the slippery slope to revolution and republicanism. Even a determined parliamentary campaign to reform the penal statutes mounted from 1810 by Sir Samuel Romilly was totally unsuccessful, his proposals being found especially unwelcome by the House of Lords.

Extreme caution and repressiveness over social matters marked English governmental policies after the defeat of France in 1815. Yet public opinion, in some measure focused by Romilly's campaigns (Romilly himself committed suicide after the death of his wife in 1818) was now alerted to the need to reform the criminal code. The commencement of national statistics on crime and punishment from 1805 allowed more informed debate, and also provide us with a background against which the campaign for reform could be placed. Certainly, the actual levels of execution in the early nineteenth century were far lower than they had been around 1600. It has been calculated, for example, that 74 persons were capitally convicted in Devon in 1598. Assuming that, as in other counties, about a fifth would be reprieved, this means that about 60 persons were executed in the county in that year. This compares with 67 persons executed in the whole of England and Wales in 1810, among them 9 murderers, 18 burglars, and 18 forgers.[48] The capital statutes for property offences became an obvious target for reformist opinion, and petitions against them and other undesirable aspects of the criminal law began to flood into parliament. On 1 March 1819 Lord Castlereagh moved for the appointment of a committee on the state of the prisons, and on the next day Sir James Mackintosh, a leading proponent of penal reform, moved for a committee on the criminal laws. Despite some opposition, a Select Committee was appointed, and its report of 1819 was a milestone in penal history. Its main objective was to collect information relating to non-violent larceny in shops or dwelling houses, and forgery, although it also explored the possibilities of a consolidation of the criminal law, and of finding the best secondary punishments with which to replace execution. Its methods pointed the way forwards towards the great parliamentary committees of the nineteenth century, with its questionnaires and its detailed argument from statistics. It recommended the abolition of a number of obsolete statutes, and the reform of the law relating to larceny and forgery. Unfortunately, these recommendations met determined opposition, and very little was actually accomplished. Nevertheless, consciousness about the need to reform the criminal code had been raised, and public opinion encouraged yet further to believe in the need for change.

This came, along with many other reforms, under Sir Robert Peel, Home Secretary from 1822. His most important measures concerning the criminal law were a series of four consolidating acts, passed between 1827 and 1830, which between them consolidated 320 acts relating to larceny and related offences, malicious damage to property, offences against the person, and forgery.[49] These and related measures, however, failed to get very far with the central issue, the dilution of the severity of the law and, in particular, the curtailing of capital punishment. A vigorous debate in pamphlets and newspapers pressed for further reform. By about 1830 opposition to the widespread use of the death penalty followed two main lines. Firstly, there was the feeling that capital punishment for property offences implied that they were as wicked as murder, an obvious absurdity. Secondly, as a number of critics of the Bloody Code argued, severe punishment was becoming counter-productive: jurors were refusing to find thieves and forgers guilty of offences which might lead to their execution, and hence thieves and forgers were going unpunished. Strikingly, there was no longer a feeling that property and social stability could only be defended by a mass of capital statutes. In this changed climate, the Bloody Code could not survive for long: by the middle of the nineteenth century public opinion had swung decisively to the view that murder was the only offence which might regularly be punished by death. The old Bloody Code was dismantled over the early years of Victoria's reign.

By the early nineteenth century, therefore, something like a watershed had been reached in the history of punishment. Offenders against the law still had to suffer, and the established notions that punishment should be about deterrence and retribution were still present. Yet the nature of punishment was changing. Capital punishment, the central weapon in the early modern struggle against crime, was being used increasingly infrequently, and was in any case being regarded as an inappropriate punishment for many of the crimes against which it had previously been employed. The old shaming punishments, such as the stocks, the pillory, carting, and ecclesiastical penance were regarded as obsolete. A new world had arrived, one which was, seemingly, full of new ideas, ideas which were to affect the punishment of criminals as much as anything else. As we shall see in the next chapter, these new ideas were to create their own anomalies, contradictions, and absurdities: any simplistic notion of 'progress' in penal policy needs to be treated with caution. Yet there was a context which was very different from that obtaining in 1550. One component of this context was the whole notion of reform: obviously, the idea of the possibility or desirability of reforming convicted criminals had been present for a long time, but now they were operating in a mental and political world which regarded reform in general terms as a good thing. Intimately connected with this feeling was the growth of the state: although still puny by modern standards, central government now desired to be infinitely more assertive in its actions, and had the means to do so. A third element was the growth of public opinion and public debate. As we have seen, by 1800 discussion of penal reform in parliament took place against a background of petitioning, pamphleteering, and argument in newspapers, while a few years later Elizabeth Fry was able to arouse the sentiments of the public and gain herself a place in the textbooks through her propaganda in favour of prison reform. Not only the punishment of criminals, but the whole of social policy, entered a new phase, a phase in which reforming groups and lobbies could achieve their ends by publicizing their position to society at large.

The arrival of this new phase should not blind us to the complexity of what had gone before. We must reiterate that the three centuries before 1800 were not some sort of arid period in which little happened before the big shifts in opinion and practice which set in after about 1775. In fact, a number of developments occurred, even if there is little evidence as to what caused them. One major shift was the massive reduction in levels of capital punishment which came in the middle of the seventeenth century. Another, less easy to quantify, was the decline in the use of shaming punishments. Despite the lack of statistics, the sense of the court archives of the period is that the stocks, carting, ecclesiastical penance and so on were less a part of the penal repertory in 1700 than they had been in 1500, a clue, perhaps, to changes in community attitudes, and in the relationship between the community and outside authority. Then there is transportation to the American colonies, haphazard at first, but then reorganized in 1718 into a system which represented a major raising of central government's involvement in crime control. And lastly, after about 1750, a quickening of interest in the use of imprisonment as a punishment. What is obvious even from a brief summary is that there was no simple unilinear development, no simple progress from barbarity to humanity. At all periods, there were contradictory trends in punishment, and little by way of either stasis or simple transitions.

The second point, connected to the first, which must be restated here, is that it is inaccurate to regard the early modern period simply as a period of unrelieved and unsystematic barbarity. Obviously, much of what happened to convicted criminals in this period would be unacceptable in any decent modern penal system: the high levels of execution, the very idea of execution for crimes other than murder, the publicity of punishment, the public stocking or carting of offenders, the more casual nastiness of many of the gaols and houses of correction of the period. Yet from 1550 onwards, and fairly consistently, the harshness of the law, and in particular the law relating to capital punishment, was being modified by the practice of the courts in favour of the offender. Moreover, many of those features of the system which seem so alien to the modern observer had their own rationale. Thus, public shaming punishments made sense in the context of a society based upon village and small town communities, public execution – as we have argued – was a more complex and more culturally significant phenomenon than many have grasped, while by the mid eighteenth century Paley and other writers were able to articulate a logical defence of the Bloody Code. Indeed, despite the emphasis that writers have put on exotic punishments and public execution, one suspects that an exhaustive search of court archives, especially if those of the local borough and manorial courts were included, would reveal the rather surprising fact that the most commonly inflicted punishment, as early as 1600, was fining. This suggestion raises some difficulties for a number of the grandiose theories about penal change in the nineteenth century, a subject which we shall address in the next chapter.

III

The Nineteenth Century

By the early nineteenth century there was evidently a growing mood in favour of reform in judicial punishment. The central issue, we must reiterate, was a profound discontent with the working of the Bloody Code. By the middle of the eighteenth century the implementation of the numerous capital statutes had become so haphazard that at least some contemporaries thought that they should be severely modified, and that offenders should be subjected to lesser punishments than death. Further disquiet, and further desires for a less haphazard and anomalous system, arose from the knowledge that a large number of those capitally convicted were subsequently pardoned, as many as two thirds in London and Middlesex in the 1790s. The courts had always attempted to mitigate the severity of the legal code, and moralists had always insisted that mercy was an integral part of justice. But by the end of the eighteenth century, a generation before the dismantling of the Bloody Code, it was evident that the implementation of capital punishment was becoming so riddled with exceptions that much of its rationale as the major force in punishment had gone. Thinking individuals set to considering the alternatives.

Most historians have concluded that the major alternative which came to hand was the prison. There is of course much to recommend such a conclusion. By the middle of the nineteenth century imprisonment had replaced capital punishment for most serious offences (murder was an obvious exception), and the image of the prison and the convict were embedded as deeply in the general culture as the public execution had been a century earlier. Some thinkers have drawn a wider moral from all this. One strand of thought, most attractive to Marxist writers, has emphasized the connection of imprisonment and the rise of industrialization, seeing symbolic (and even architectural) links between the prison and the factory.[1] More recently, Foucault (1977) and Ignatieff (1978) have argued that much deeper changes were symbolized in the rise of the prison. Foucault's opinions have proved particularly influential, forming as they did one facet of that philosopher's broader intellectual schema. Foucault saw in the transition from the 'public' punishment on the scaffold to the 'private' punishment of the prison an epitome of the differences by which power operated in the pre-industrial and the modern world. The target of punishment (and hence of the exercising of power) was now control of the soul of the offender, rather than his or her body. The connected changes in penal technology led to new ideas on crime and the criminal, and ultimately resulted the current situation where crime and punishment are not just matters for judges, jurors, hangmen and gaolers, but also 'experts' – psychologists, criminologists, social workers, probation officers. More generally, Foucault argues, this change is entwined with the way in which power operates in the modern world: physical force is replaced by power founded on detailed knowledge, routine intervention, and upon regulation rather than random repression.

The Hulks and Transportation

All of this would have seemed very distant and totally unpredictable in the England of the 1780s, where a crisis of major proportions was forcing those running the system of punishment to concentrate on rather shorter term problems. The end of the American War, and with it the end of transportation to the American colonies, meant that the law enforcement system had to regulate the expedients it had employed to dispose of convicted criminals over the past seven years. The first of these came in 1776 when the first disruption of transportation which the troubles in the colonies had caused had stimulated an Act 'to authorise . . . the punishment of hard labour' for offenders who would normally have been transported, the hard labour in question being cleansing and improving the navigation of the River Thames. Women, and men incapable of performing such work, were to be sent to houses of correction, where they were to be separated from the other inmates and set to hard labour. Thus the 1776 Act, to quote John Beattie, 'adopted and extended the practice of imprisoning noncapital convicts at hard labour that the assize judges had accepted for some offenders as the problems with transportation developed,'[2] a practice which had grown gradually over the previous twenty years. As such, it helped establish imprisonment with hard labour as a standard punishment for felony, which in turn pointed towards later developments. It also introduced one of the most unsavoury penal institutions ever employed in England: the prison hulks.

The 1776 Act gave no indication of where the prisoners who were employed at hard labour in cleansing the Thames were actually to be kept, although it did direct that they should be placed under an overseer who was to be appointed by the Middlesex justices. The overseer was to contract to take the convicts off the government's hands, appoint and pay his own supervisory staff, and organize the prisoners' accommodation. The first overseer was Duncan Campbell, who had held the last contract for transporting convicted criminals to the colonies. He built on his previous expertise by anchoring two ships, the *Justitia* and the *Censor*, near Woolwich in August 1776 and placing 300 prisoners on them. These were to be loaded, in chains, onto lighters every morning, and sent to work along the Thames. Later another hulk and a hospital ship joined them, while other vessels were placed at Plymouth and Portsmouth. Thereafter, the number of hulks and those incarcerated within them varied. In 1815 there were five hulks holding 2,429 convicts, in 1828 ten holding 4,446, in 1850 four holding around 2,000.

From 1814 until 1847 the hulks were under the control of John Capper, a relatively efficient administrator who introduced closer supervision over the inmates in the hulks, and who also attempted to classify them into various categories, the most notable result of this being the designation of certain hulks for young offenders. The system was exported, with hulks being established at Bermuda in 1824, Ireland in 1826, and Gibraltar in 1842. But by 1847 opinion was hardening against the hulks, and attacks upon them were mounted in the House of Commons. This growing disquiet at the conditions on the hulks, allied to the practical problems of maintaining them (some were literally falling to pieces) led to the discontinuation of their use in England in 1857.

The hulks did much to accustom the public mind to the notion that incarceration with hard labour might be an appropriate punishment for crime, while the practices adopted to manage the prisoners on the hulks in many ways anticipated aspects of what went on in the later penitentiaries. Yet (and making due allowance for the partiality of many of the sources) conditions on the hulks, and especially in the early days of their use, were appalling. No complete figures for convict mortality have ever been calculated, but it seems that initially something like a third of those incarcerated in the hulks died in them. Their bodies were buried in unconsecrated ground along the banks of the Thames, or sent for dissection, a sideline which, according to one former prisoner, earned the hulk doctors £5 or £6 a corpse. Supervision of prisoners overnight was impossible: they were simply battened down and left to their own devices. Bullying among the prisoners was incessant, while James Hardy Vaux, a gentleman thief imprisoned on the hulks at the end of the eighteenth century, recorded that robbery among the convicts was 'as common as cursing', that during his incarceration he witnessed deliberate murder and suicide, and that 'unnatural crimes are openly committed'.[3] Convicts on the *Portland*, according to the captain, spent the night 'making money, hammering out crowns and half crowns into sixpences'.[4] The guards themselves, according to Vaux, were 'commonly of the lowest class of human beings; wretches devoid of all feeling; ignorant in the extreme, brutal by nature, and rendered tyrannical and cruel by the consciousness of the power they possess'.[5] It is little surprise that those serving their time in the hulks normally left them worse than they entered them. As early as 1785 the Committee on Transportation noted that the hulks 'Form distinct societies for the complete instruction of all newcomers', and that convicts leaving them 'return to the mass of the community, not reformed in their principles but confirmed in every vicious habit'.[6]

Nevertheless the hulks, before they were finally phased out of the British penal system in 1857, did ease the pressure on that system. In particular, they helped weaken the trend towards higher levels of executions which set in immediately after the disruption of transportation in 1776. This crisis also prompted a search for other solutions. A House of Commons committee considered a number of measures, among them the establishment of penal colonies on the coast of West Africa, or, as Joseph Banks, who had sailed with Captain Cook, suggested, at Botany Bay in recently mapped Australia. The courts continued to pass sentences of transportation, even though there was nowhere to send convicts, although an Act of 1784 allowing convicts under sentence of transportation to be placed on the hulks did at least ease the pressure on county gaols. Various plans continued to be broached (purchasing Greenland and founding a penal colony there was one suggestion), but in 1786 the cabinet agreed to settle a colony at Botany Bay. Das Voltas Bay, by the mouth of the Orange River in South West Africa, had initially seemed more viable: it would have been cheaper to send convicts there, and it was of greater strategic significance. But a survey ship reported that the place was too barren to be settled, and the cabinet fell back on Botany Bay. No proper survey had been carried out of that location, but by now the congestion of convicts in prisons, bridewells and the hulks was overwhelming. Without a proper survey of the area to be settled, without any proper knowledge of the Australian continent, despite the costs of transporting convicts there, the government decided to set up a penal colony at Botany Bay.[7]

The first fleet landed at Botany Bay at 10 a.m. on 20 January 1788. The last convict ship to arrive in Australia, the *Hougoumont*, landed 279 convicts, a few Fenian Irishmen among them, at Freemantle in January 1868. Over this eighty-year period some 160,000 British and Irish convicts were transported to Australia, a majority to New South Wales, some to Van Diemen's Land (the modern Tasmania), and, from 1829, about 9,668 to Western Australia. Of the total 24,960 (just under a sixth) were women, 80 per cent of them sent out for theft. Perhaps 11,800 convicts were transported between 1787 and 1811, the Napoleonic Wars cutting back the early exodus. With the ending of those wars the numbers sent out rose rapidly: between 1787 and 1811, some 17,400; some 32,800 between 1821 and 1830; another 51,200 in the 1840s; 26,000 in the 1850s, mainly to Van Diemen's Land; with the remainder, most of them going to Western Australia, between 1826 and the ending of transportation in 1868.

The voyage was a long one, usually taking about 110 days, with most captains sailing down to Rio, and then proceeding straight across to Australia. Fatalities on the voyage were not as high as might have been expected: some of the early fleets suffered heavy mortality, but in the peak years of the system only 1 per cent of convicts died in transit. This was just as well, given the costs involved (but see Lewis, 1988). Transportation cost £579,000 over the years 1810–12, a remarkable investment for the period, and by the 1840s was running at between £400,000 and £500,000 a year. Over the period in which the system was in operation, however, the average cost of transportation per convict fell drastically, from £100 to £30.

The first fleet, understandably, has attracted special attention, both because of its marking a novel departure in penal practice, and on account of its crucial role in Australian history. Its commander, Captain Arthur Phillip, was an undistinguished but perfectly competent career officer aged forty-eight, who was probably appointed because in a period of service with the Portuguese navy he had captained a boatload of convicts across the Atlantic to Brazil without the loss of one of them. In the event, he proved a very capable commander of the convict fleet, losing far fewer convicts in transit than did the two fleets which followed his, and was also a capable commander of the new penal colony. His fleet left England with 736 convicts, 548 of them men, 188 women. They came from most parts of England, although the largest single group among them had been convicted in courts in and around London. Their average age was twenty-seven, although they included in their number Dorothy Holland, aged eighty-two, and John Hudson, aged nine. The overwhelming majority of them, like the young Hudson, were transported for property offences, 431 of them for larceny. The fleet consisted of eleven vessels, two of them naval warships, three storeships, and six transports. The largest was the *Alexander* (452 tons) which was 114 ft long and 31 ft wide, and was supposed to carry 210 convicts. Phillip brought his fleet and its human cargo (the crews and the marines who were to form the disciplinary presence in the new colony roughly equalled the convicts in number) over in good order to Botany Bay, but found the place, despite the reports he had received, unsuitable for a colony. A search was made up the coast, and a landing place was found at what was soon to be known as Sydney Harbour.

The difficulties of the enterprise which Phillip found himself commanding should not be underestimated. Convicted felons had been transported before, to the American colonies to take the obvious example. But these had gone to developing societies and had been assimilated into ever increasing numbers of free settlers. Phillip and those under him were starting from scratch, and were placed in the most geographically distant colony in the British Empire. The early years, as the colony established itself in an alien environment with little by way of skilled labour, tools and equipment, and insufficient supplies from home, saw hardship, disease, and near starvation. The second fleet arrived in 1790, the third in 1791, both of them carrying numerous sick convicts who added to the burdens of the colony. The second fleet also brought two companies of the New South Wales Corps, which was to become a serious political force in the early years of the colony. Things were tight for the first few years of the colony's existence, but by the end of 1791 it at least seemed probable that Sydney would be able to support itself. Free settlers were very rare at this early stage, but Phillip supported the granting of land to convicts deemed worthy of it. Most time-expired convicts, however, seemed happy to work their passage back to England in the early days. At the end of 1792 Phillip, upon whom the colony's survival had depended in the first phase, sailed home and joined them.

The other main convict colony was Van Diemen's Land, occupied in 1803. The initial party consisted of 25 free settlers and New South Wales Corps personnel, and 24 convicts. Two ships arrived from England later in the year, and the convicts they landed joined with the earlier party to settle the site of what was eventually to become Hobart. Like their predecessors at Sydney, they suffered hardship, disease and near starvation in the early stages of the settlement and owed their early survival to kangaroo hunting. This in turn led them into conflict with the island's original inhabitants for this scant resource: the subsequent deliberate extermination of Van Diemen's Land's aborigines was one of the most shameful episodes in the history of Britain's colonial expansion. Yet here, too, the early difficulties were overcome, and convicts were to come to form a very high proportion of Van Diemen's Land's population: they formed 58 per cent in 1832, and 34.4 per cent in 1847, by which time the proportion of convicts in New South Wales had fallen to 3.2 per cent. The island, however, had a reputation for being tough on convicts, largely because of the early penal settlement at Port Arthur, and the 'Place of Ultra Banishment and Punishment', founded at Macquarie Harbour in 1821 for convicts who had committed a second offence in the colony. In 1824 Van Diemen's Land was officially set up as a colony, its first governor being Sir George Arthur, an autocrat who was determined to turn the island into the epitome of a penal colony. Yet his governership was efficient, and many of Arthur's measures (for example his insistence that prisoners could receive graduated rewards for good behaviour) was in keeping with the best contemporary penal theory. Later governors were less successful, and under Sir John Eardley Eardley-Wilmot, appointed in 1843, the convict system on the island more or less fell to pieces, and free settlers left in large numbers. Eardley-Wilmot was dismissed in 1846, helped on his way by the outrage generated in Britain by reports of homosexuality among the convicts placed under his charge and transportation to Van Diemen's Land was temporarily suspended.

The experiences of the 160,000 convicts who went out to Australia, sentenced for seven, ten, fourteen years or life were varied. As the colonies grew, convict labour became a vital component of the economy, and many convicts found themselves working in farms or workshops. Those who found themselves under good masters and were capable of reforming their ways might profit from the experience of life in a new land, and lead a useful existence when they had finished their sentence. The occasional success story that such convicts might generate led many commentators to claim that Australia was an easy option for convicts, and odd comments by criminals in England suggest that such sentiments were not totally unknown among the lower orders. As early as 1788 thirteen-year-old William Floyd was supposed to have told the constable who arrested him that 'they can't hang us . . . we shall only go to Botany Bay for seven years, and that at my age will soon whip away'.[8] Had he gone out a few decades later, he would have found a few nasty surprises waiting for him. As the Molesworth

Committee reported in 1837, it was by then a regular practice for newly arrived boy convicts to be sexually abused by their older fellows. The risks of punishment under convict discipline were added to those of sodomy. By the 1830s there were 22,000 summary convictions in New South Wales among 28,000 convicts, 3,000 of whom were flogged a total of 108,000 lashes, mainly for insolence, insubordination, and neglecting their work. Chain gangs both there and in Van Diemen's Land were simply locked up in overcrowded 'caravans' or 'boxes' overnight. Conditions in the punishment stations of Norfolk Island and Port Arthur were apparently terrible. In 1834, after a mutiny in the former, a Catholic priest comforting those who had been condemned to death for their participation read out the names of those who were to be executed, who 'one after the other, as their names were pronounced, dropped on their knees and thanked God that they were to be delivered from that terrible place'.[9] The priest in question, William Ullathorne, was later a leading witness in the inquiries which led to the end of transportation to New South Wales.

Transportation aroused a whole spectrum of criticisms. As we have noted, there was one line of thought which considered it to be too light a punishment, in that it offered convicts the eventual chance of making good in a new country, and thus perhaps enjoying better opportunities than the labouring classes in Britain. At the same time, as is so often the case when penal policy is under discussion, another body of opinion held that it was too severe, and led to the degradation and demoralization of the convict. Transportation might also have been presented as causing that pain of uprooting, and of the breaking of social ties, associated with the punishment of 'exile' in tsarist Russia. As reformist ideas became fashionable, their proponents, the odd story of a convict making good notwithstanding, could find little to encourage them in the experience of convicts in Australia: the contribution of convicts to crime in their new environment certainly did little to support the view that their experience of punishment was making them better citizens. Evidence could, of course, be found to support either view, which could lead to a very logical third objection to transportation, that the very uncertainty of its effects rendered it dubious as a punishment. It was doubtless effective in its prime role, that of removing felons (and, perhaps, the core of the criminal classes of future generations) from Britain. But it was very uncertain if it did very much by way of deterrence, while a steady flow of information from the colonies also suggested that it was doing little by way of reformation. This information was also suggesting that the normal convict life of the colonies was extremely harsh and brutal. More seriously, perhaps, the system, most dramatically in Van Diemen's Land, was showing signs of severe malfunction.

Opposition to transportation gained considerable focus in the Molesworth Committee of 1837. Like most parliamentary committees of the period, this body was anxious to find evidence to support its biases (Molesworth himself was anti-transportationist) and its deliberations have recently been characterized as 'a heavily biased show trial designed to present a catalogue of antipodean horrors, conducted by Whigs against a system they were already planning to jettison'.[10] British public opinion was enraged when the Committee's findings were published, and transportation to New South Wales more or less came to an end. Amidst continued debate, both in Britain and Australia (by this stage a steady flow of voluntary immigrants were arriving in Australia, and some people of influence there were beginning to resent having to accept the motherland's more deviant offspring), transportation to Van Diemen's Land ended in the 1850s, and the last boatload of convicts for Western Australia landed in 1868. The whole Australian transportation project was a remarkable one, and constituted one of the few occasions when a penal experiment led to the founding of a new nation.

It was also remarkable in involving a heavy outlay of government money, not least because it rapidly became obvious that hopes of the convict colonies offsetting this by proving economically beneficial to Britain were proving over-optimistic. Early plans for jute production, for example, came to nothing. Yet after 1792 New South Wales was at least self-sufficient in foodstuffs, and a healthy farming sector, heavily dependent on convict labour, came into being. As the population of free or emancipated settlers grew, so too did the number of small farms. Convicts were assigned to free settlers and, if they stayed with the same master for a continuous period, might earn freedom on a 'ticket of leave' after four to eight years, depending on the length of their original sentence. As we have noted, the fate of the convict under that assignment system might depend very heavily on the nature of the settler to whom he was assigned. Another anomalous area was created by sending convicts into public works, a practice in some sense presaging the labour camps of the twentieth century. This was, perhaps, at its most marked under Lachlan Macquarie, Governor of New South Wales from January 1810 to December 1821. Macquarie was an able and constructive governor (in fact, he was replaced partly because he was thought to be too soft on convicts) who was determined to put the colony on a sound footing. Part of his plan included the construction of a number of public buildings, ranging from convict 'factories' to churches. Most of these were designed by a convict architect, Francis Howard Greenway (there was no free architect in New South Wales at the time), and they were celebrated in verse by a convict poet, Michael Massey Robinson. More prosaically, Macquarie's schemes meant that a large number of convicts, including almost all of those with a skill, were working for the government rather than for settlers. This caused some resentment, and after 1821 the proportion of convicts working on government projects fell.

The history of the hulks and of transportation constitutes more than a mere byway from what many have considered the main theme of punishment after 1780, the rise of the prison. The hulks fostered both some of the public attitudes and some of the managerial practices which were involved in the rise of the penitentiary prison. They also provide a classic example of that recurring phenomenon in penal history, the temporary expedient that becomes a part of the structure of things: originally envisaged as something which would be used for two years as a stopgap, the hulks were in use for nearly eighty, although this use was declining well before their final demise. With the history of transportation we encounter yet more evidence of how public opinion, sometimes orchestrated by interested parties, had come to be such a force in the early nineteenth century. The decision to send convicts to Australia, although taken in a period of crisis in the system of punishment, was essentially a continuation of a long established practice: indeed, exile, in a sense the ancestor of transportation as a punishment, had been known in the ancient world.

The initial impetus for transportation to Australia was the established one of eliminating criminals from Britain. Growing concern over the existence of a self-reproducing 'criminal class' led some observers to take this idea a stage further, and argue that transportation ridded Britain of future habitual criminals as well as the current ones. Yet by the time of the Molesworth Committee it is evident that a powerful body of opinion could no longer regard simple elimination as a viable option. There were considerable doubts about the deterrent effect of transportation, there was a strong feeling that it did not reform, and sensibilities were ruffled by accounts of the conditions under which many convicts existed. The system, moreover, was becoming increasingly difficult to administer, both from London and in the colonies. The history of transportation, therefore, provides a microcosm of how attitudes to judicial punishment, and the levels of sophistication of debate about such matters, changed in the fifty years after 1776.

The Prison

The prison had traditionally, as far as felons were concerned, been the place where suspects were held before trial rather than a place where criminals were punished. Prisons were also, traditionally, run by the sheriff, who would normally sub-contract their day-to-day operation to the gaoler. But by the late seventeenth century the county justices were increasingly taking the administration of the county gaol under their direct control (houses of correction were also run under the aegis of the bench), while by the eighteenth the imprisonment of convicted felons was becoming an accepted part of local penal practice. Conditions in county gaols, borough prisons, and local houses of correction varied enormously. Some were ramshackle structures likely to aid neither the secure incarceration nor the physical well-being of their inmates. Such institutions were made worse if the gaoler, who was in any case dependent on fees from prisoners for his income, was brutal, negligent, or extortionate. Others were much better. In 1777, however, the English prison system was damned irrevocably by the publication of John

Howard's *The State of the Prisons*, regarded by many as the fundamental text of penal reform. Howard's book, based on impressive researches, had a massive impact on a public consciousness which was, as we have noted, already alert to the need to do something about prisons.[11] This need was seen as being all the more pressing as the gaols suffered from recurrent outbreaks of gaol fever, and became more overcrowded as the American War of Independence made transportation temporarily impossible. Typically, the first experiment in gaol reform was based on a local initiative, when the Sussex justices under the guidance of the Duke of Richmond decided to erect a new county gaol at Horsham. Probably inspired by the Rasp House at Amsterdam and the Maison de Force at Ghent, this was completed in 1779. Its regulations did not envisage the reforming objectives or prison work which were to be the hallmarks of the early nineteenth-century penitentiary. The rules did, however, inaugurate a salaried staff rather than one dependent on fees, outside inspection, and a proper diet and other necessities for prisoners. Interestingly the Sussex scheme envisaged the employment of a prison chaplain at £50 a year. It also involved the dispersion of prisoners into separate cells at night.

By this point early signs of a movement for penal reform were beginning to manifest themselves on a national level, and in 1779 Howard and his associates managed to get legislation to establish a national penitentiary through parliament, although no practical consequences followed. The 1780s, however, were to see a number of further local experiments in penal reform, notably in Gloucestershire, where five new houses of correction and a county gaol were opened in 1792 at a cost of £46,000. The moving force here was the local sheriff, Sir George Onesiphorus Paul. With its reformatory ideal, Paul's penitentiary looked forward to nineteenth-century developments. Paul regarded imprisonment as a punishment of the mind rather than the body: solitary confinement, scanty food and hard labour would reduce the prisoner to a state of mind in which religion could reform him. This ideal spread in educated circles, the only real challenge among reformers coming from Jeremy Bentham. Bentham envisaged a prison which would enjoy a severe regime, the only limitation being that the prisoners' health should not be endangered. Conditions for prisoners were to be roughly equivalent to those experienced by the poor outside, and the prison should be self-supporting due to the profits of convict labour: indeed, Bentham envisaged himself running the prison for a fee and a percentage of what the prisoners earned. Perhaps the most remarkable feature of Bentham's ideas, revealed in 1791, was his design for a prison, a 'Panopticon' which would allow a centrally placed observer to survey the inmates. Although his overall plans were rejected by the strongly reformatory mood of the period, his notions on prison architecture attracted considerable interest. This interest, however, was not much translated into the actual construction of gaols in Britain: Bentham's Panopticon has had a greater impact on later historians than it did on the practical policies of his contemporaries.

The idea of reforming the prisoner was central to a major statement of penal policy, the report of the Holford Committee in 1811. Following this report, which again pointed the way forwards to a number of later developments, a national penitentiary was built at Millbank, on the site currently occupied by the Tate Gallery. Completed in 1816, at a cost, according to some estimates, of £500,000, its wall enclosed seven acres of buildings and nine of gardens: the corridors along which its cells were placed ran for three miles, and 860 prisoners (or at a push 1,000) could be kept there at an average cost in 1829 of £30 3s. each a year. The prisoners were kept in separate cells, although they were able to associate during the day. They were also to work, although any pretence at training withered as the number of trades taught shrank to one, weaving. Millbank employed an extensive staff, the whole supervised by a Committee of Management. There was a governor, a chaplain, a schoolteacher, a matron, a surgeon, and sixty to eighty subordinate officers. Together the staff were to be responsible for the health, moral welfare and reform of the prisoners as well as their incarceration. The size of the undertaking and the break it represented with past procedures was immense. Millbank did not just represent a new dimension in punishment: it was also symbolic of a broader change in the relationship between the individual and the state.

Central government interest in prisons continued to grow as the nineteenth century progressed, partly as a result of the continued efforts of a small group of reformers, partly in response to public fears over what was seen as an ever growing crime problem. In 1835 legislation aimed at ensuring a greater uniformity of practice in prisons in England and Wales, and to that end appointed Prison Commissioners. These represented a considerable intrusion into what had previously been a local government concern, perhaps the most important addition to their ranks in the early days being Captain Joshua Jebb, a Royal Engineers officer who was made Surveyor-General of Prisons in 1839. In 1837 the Molesworth Committee's recommendation that transportation to Van Diemen's Land should be ended and replaced by hard labour at home obviously lent a certain urgency to the problem of prison construction and administration. In 1838 Parkhurst Gaol was established for juvenile offenders, and in 1842 legislation was passed providing for the construction of a prison for adult inmates which was to stand as the epitome of the penitentiary system: Pentonville. It was to cost £84,000 to construct and was to hold 520 prisoners. Within its 25-ft wall was a six acre site. Within its buildings were the convicts' cells, each of them 13½ ft long, 7½ ft wide, 9 ft high. There the convicts, in the early days, were to spend 18 months in solitary confinement (the period was soon cut: too many prisoners went mad or committed suicide) before being transported or, later, sent to a public works prison. They were to breakfast on cocoa and bread, lunch on gruel, dine on stew, receive regular moral instruction via the chapel, and be allowed to send one letter a week. Pentonville, even more than Millbank, was symbolic of the new penal cosmos: 'In a way which no prison today could ever be,' wrote Michael Ignatieff, 'it was both a focal point of public debate and one of the monuments of the day.'[12]

One factor in this public debate, as we have hinted, was concern over levels of crime.[13] However mistakenly, a substantial body of opinion was, by about 1830, convinced that something like a breakdown of a social order was imminent, and that a solution to the crime problem was a necessary guarantee against such an eventuality. Within this general public concern a more specialized debate over proposals for prison reform had been running for some time. Leaving aside Bentham's proposals, which attracted little attention, two systems of prison administration were contesting for public and official support, both of them American in origin. The first of these was the solitary confinement (or separate) regime used in Philadelphia, the second the silent associated system used at Auburn and Sing Sing prisons. In the former, prisoners were kept for up to five years in total seclusion, their solitary life broken only by visits from prison staff. The Auburn system involved prisoners being kept alone in cells overnight, but being allowed to work together, yet in strict silence, during the day. It was the separate system which eventually won approval among England's penal policy-makers, and which was to form the basis of the regime at Pentonville. The length of solitary confinement was rapidly cut to twelve and then eight months as its impact on the prisoners' sanity was realized. With this minor modification, the Pentonville model was regarded as a great success: by 1850, ten new prisons had been built following it, and another ten had been converted to the separate system. At the basis of the separate system, it must be reiterated, was the optimistic and progressive notion of reforming the prisoner. Left to himself with ample time to reflect on the way of life that had brought him to this pass, the prisoner would be all the more open to the message of the Bible in his cell and the prison chaplain. Ignatieff has argued that there was a yet deeper significance of the penitentiary ideal. It appealed in the early nineteenth century not just because of its 'functional capacity to control crime',

> but rather because the reformers presented it as a response, not merely to crime, but to the whole social crisis of a period, and as part of a larger strategy of political, social, and legal reform designed to reestablish order on a new foundation.[14]

By about 1860, however, the penitentiary prison was taken more or less for granted, and the fears of social breakdown had gone. Curiously, the idea that the basic function of the prison was to reform the offender seems to have gone with them.

Concentration on the brave new world of central government's penitentiaries should not obscure the fact that most prisons in England and Wales were smaller institutions with less grandiose objectives run by local authorities.[15] Estimates of their number vary. James Nield thought that there were 317 in 1812, while parliamentary returns suggested that there were 335 in the United

Kingdom in 1819 and 291 in 1833.[16] Despite extensive rebuilding and efficient regimes in many of these prisons, not all of the eighteenth-century problems had been eradicated. Even the effectively run ones were far from total institutions on the Pentonville model, while if a local prison was redesigned, it tended to be the silent rather than the separate system which was adopted: the latter was more expensive to operate. By about 1850, however, many of the very small local prisons and bridewells had been closed, while those which remained were usually well regulated. Conditions in the local prisons were undoubtedly varied, but it does seem that after about 1860 governors of local prisons were beginning to share those harsher ideas about prison regimes which were apparent in the running of the penitentiaries.

In 1850 the Board of Directors of Convict Prisons was set up, with Sir Joshua Jebb as its chairman, a post he was to hold until 1863 when he died on the upper deck of the bus taking him to the office. His main effort, as transportation ground towards discontinuation, was to find a formula by which sentences in prisons could be made equivalent to the older terms of transportation. He estimated that four years of the former was equal to seven years of the latter, although the Penal Servitude Act of 1865 was to prescribe a minimum of five years penal servitude, with seven for anybody previously convicted of felony. Generally, there was a feeling in the early 1860s that the existing system of penal servitude was not harsh enough.

On Jebb's death he was succeeded by Edmund Henderson, another Royal Engineers officer, who was replaced in turn by yet another Royal Engineer, Edmund Du Cane, in 1869. Du Cane, as Chairman of the Directors of Convict Prisons, Inspector-General of Military Prisons, and Surveyor-General of Prisons was, up to his retirement in 1895, to have complete control of the convict prison system, and combined these responsibilities with being Chairman of the Prison Commissioners. Du Cane was a hard-liner who thought that punishment was more important than reformation. Accordingly, although the basics of penal servitude were much the same under his regime (nine months' solitary at Pentonville or Millbank, then the remainder of the sentence at a public works or 'invalid' prison) the experience was made tougher. Education and training were cut, the role of the chaplain curtailed, diets made more frugal and less appealing, and the flogging of convicts for disciplinary offences within the prison became more common. Above all, the prison system under Du Cane was run with as little regard for public opinion and with as little recourse to public scrutiny as possible.

Du Cane's greatest achievement, however, was to preside over the integration of the local and the convict prisons into one unified system, firmly under his control. For its supporters, this operation was one of rationalization. Uniformity could now be imposed on prison discipline, prisons could be funded by central government rather than by the local rates, and costs could be cut by closing the smaller local gaols. Opposition came mainly from those bent on defending local interests against an ever encroaching central government. Despite this opposition, the bill gained the royal assent in July 1877, coming into operation the following spring. There had been a number of important acts relating to prisons during the nineteenth century, of which the legislation of 1865 was especially significant, but the 1877 Act was crucial in laying the foundations of the future system. Its most immediate effect, however, was the slimming down of the local gaols: something like fifty of the 116 local prisons were closed fairly rapidly, and the consequent streamlined system was unified under the tight control of Du Cane.

Du Cane's regime, however, inevitably provoked a reaction. In 1893, after severe criticism in the national press, a full-scale campaign was launched against him, with William Douglas Morris, chaplain of Wandsworth prison, taking a leading part. In 1894 Herbert Gladstone (the son of W. E.) was appointed chairman of a parliamentary committee on prisons. The Gladstone Committee's report offered a major reversal of the previous regime. Deterrence was seen as a vital aspect of imprisonment, but reformation was reinstated as having a central role. There was a notion of 'individualization of treatment'. Ever since the days of John Howard there had been an awareness that all prisoners were not the same, and that they should be grouped into different classes. The Gladstone Committee envisaged a more elaborate system of classification of prisoners into categories of 'like natures', rejected the rigid adherence to the separate system, criticized useless hard labour in the local prisons, and advised that a local interest in these institutions should be maintained by visiting committees. The subsequent Prison Act of 1898, despite its difficult passage through parliament, reasserted the importance of reformation as an objective, and offered a number of ameliorations to the prisoner's everyday existence. The way now seemed open for the more optimistic and progressive penal regime of the early twentieth century.

The legislative and administrative history of prisons in this period, essentially the view 'from above', is, of course, only part of the story. Nineteenth-century penal policy affected prisoners (and, indeed, prison staff) as well as prisons. There are tremendous problems involved in attempting to grasp the realities of prison life, especially in the pre-Victorian era. It is all too easy to caricature prison conditions in the eighteenth century, yet both the proponents of reform and more neutral commentators were united in their comments. Not only, it would seem, did prisoners live in bad physical conditions: the moral climate of the carceral institutions of the period was also distinctly unedifying. Jacob Ilive, a London bookseller sent to Clerkenwell House of Correction for libel in 1757, has left us a neat portrayal of the state of affairs which so disturbed John Howard, Jeremy Bentham and the rest. Ilive

> observed a great number of dirty young wenches intermixed with some men, some felons who had fetters on, sitting on the ground against the wall, sunning and lousing themselves; others lying sound asleep; some sleeping with their faces in men's laps, and some men doing the same by the women. I found on enquiry that these women, most of them, were sent hither by the justices as loose and disorderly persons.[17]

The inmates, Ilive recorded, spent their time in drinking and gaming together, or indulging in such pastimes as the 'very merry, but abominably obscene' game of 'rowly powly' (Ilive's sensibilities prevented him from noting the details of this recreational pursuit). Other gaols, notably Newgate, which received considerable criticism from reformers, possessed a fully developed prisoner subculture, while at the Fleet the debtors practically ran the prison.[18] As ever, conditions varied massively between prisons and prisoners, but in a large prison with an agreeable gaoler an inmate with money and friends outside could live well, and enjoy easy access to food, drink and sexual outlets.

All of this was to change as the new prison regimes came in from the late eighteenth century. Perhaps the greatest change, and one that is so obvious that it is easy to lose sight of, is that the boundaries between the prison and the outside world became absolute. We now have much less opportunity for finding out what goes on in prisons than did John Howard, simply because the world of the prison and the prisoner has been so separated from ours. Other important changes revolved around the placing of the moral reform of the offenders at the head of the agenda. As a result of this, solitary confinement, during which prisoners could contemplate their sinful past and their more law-abiding future, replaced the continual prisoner contacts of the old prison. Late eighteenth-century reformers saw the confusion of prisoner categories described by Ilive as one of the main obstacles to the implementation of reform and proper prison discipline and were particularly keen to separate male offenders from female ones, young ones from adult ones, and criminals from debtors. The new discipline experienced first in the penitentiaries and then throughout the prison system implied the categorization of prisoners: by the nature of their offence, by their previous record, by their conduct within the prison, by the hopes of their being reformed, by age, by sex. It is no accident that the prison system in its modern sense emerged at the same time as did the modern discipline of social science. Understanding society now meant forming models, forming analyses. What group in society was a more obvious target for these processes than the inmates of prisons? As Foucault observed, constructing a typology of prisoners is considerably easier once you actually have them in the prison: above all, they can be used as the basis for data which allows criminals and penology to be approached 'scientifically'. Nineteenth-century penal policy and penal practices were aspects of much wider social and intellectual processes.[19]

For the historian, perhaps the most welcome facet of the Victorian prison system is that for the first time the opinions of those on the receiving end of punishment are available in reasonable quantities. The prison and its inmates soon became objects of fascination to the non-criminal public, and as part of this process Victorian and

Edwardian readers were regaled with the memoirs of pseudononymous ex-prisoners: 'Convict 77'; 'Half-Timer'; 'Ticket of Leave Man'; 'One who has endured it'; 'One who has tried them', and so on.[20] Indeed, by the late nineteenth century the convict and the prison were firmly lodged in the wider popular consciousness. The increasingly popular detective novels of the period, its sentimental monologues, even music-hall sketches, all fixed the image of the convict firmly in the broader culture. The enduring image of the convict, the cropped-haired man in the broad-arrow uniform, is essentially a legacy of the late Victorian era.

These convict memoirs give a view of prison life which is very different from that provided by government reports and other forms of official documentation. Prisoners are not, of course, inherently any more likely than prison officers, prison governors or prison commissioners to give impartial accounts of prison life. Even so, their accounts make fascinating reading. They agree that entry into the prison, especially for first-timers, was a shock to the system, and one which was inherently dehumanizing. On arrival the convicts would give up their property and clothing, be bathed (not always in the most salubrious of conditions) and then be provided with prison clothing (this varied: local prisons favoured parti-coloured garments, while in convict prisons the broad-arrow uniform was current by the 1870s). There would then be a medical inspection and, for men, a haircut, 'as close as the scissors can go: them's the governor's orders', as 'One who has tried them' described it in 1881.[21] Convicts were given a number, and might have the prison rules read out to them by a warder. They would then be conducted to their cell, which would be equipped with a bed (or at least planks), eating utensils, some cleaning equipment, a coarse towel and some soap, a chair and a table, a Bible, a prayer book, and a copy of *Hymns Ancient and Modern*. The cell was cold and was, of course, normally solitary: prison memoirs recorded the keeping of flies, spiders, rats, mice, even a blackbird as pets to ease the solitude.

The daily round for the prisoner began at 5 or 6 a.m. with slopping out and cleaning the cell. Chapel would follow, with the separate system still being enforced in some prisons even as the prisoners attended services. The prisoners' memoirs are unanimous that prison food was atrocious. The main elements in the diet were bread and gruel (or 'stirabout'), the latter a porridge of oatmeal and indian meal. Potatoes, meat and soup would also be provided, although the potatoes were frequently rotten and the meat and soup of an appalling quality. Scurvy was still common in prisons in 1899, while many prisoners suffered from digestive or dietary ailments. Adverse comment by prisoners on their food, like most of their complaints, was met by the less-eligibility argument: there was no reason why prisoners should be better fed than free paupers. The end of the day brought little relief, for many prisoners remembered insomnia as one of the problems regularly experienced. This problem was made worse by the practice, recommended in 1863, of providing prisoners serving short sentences or the early stages of long ones not with a bed, but merely with planks to sleep on. Stuart Wood, a petty criminal who served many sentences early in the twentieth century, claimed that insomnia turned many male convicts into 'that pitiful thing – the habitual masturbate', noting that 'one finally yields to temptation in the hope of obtaining sleep'.[22]

There was a general consensus that during their waking hours prisoners should work, but there was also considerable confusion as to what exactly this should entail. Bentham, it will be remembered, had suggested that prisoners should labour usefully so as to defray the costs of their incarceration, while the proponents of the reformatory approach saw work as an intrinsically good thing in moral terms: the experience of labour would aid reformation, while the learning of a trade might help the prisoner to obtain employment on release. In the event, attempts to give prisoners useful training or work experience were few and far between, while initiatives in this respect were rarely sustained for any length of time. Early in the nineteenth century picking oakum (i.e. obtaining a loose fibre used in caulking ships or stopping leaks by untwisting old rope) was a standard form of prison work, a more or less pointless activity which, as one recent writer put it, was retained 'because of its simplicity and its tediousness and because no one could think of a better way of keeping so many unskilled hands from idleness'.[23] Any reformatory ideas were more or less dropped in the 1860s, when it was decided that prison work should be fully penal: if prisoners enjoyed or benefited from it, it was failing in its object.

The nineteenth century was to see a number of experiments in 'work' in prison which clearly fulfilled no useful function. The most celebrated of these was the treadwheel, apparently invented by William Cubitt, a civil engineer from Norfolk, after a visit to Bury St Edmunds gaol in 1818. This device was occasionally used to pump water or grind corn, but more often the prisoners working the wheel were engaged in the utterly pointless task of 'grinding air'. One recommendation was that a prisoner should do the equivalent of turning the wheel 12,000 feet a day, roughly the equivalent of climbing the Matterhorn. Similar use was made of the crank, a wheel set against cogs which had a resisting pressure, turned by a handle which could have weights attached to it to make the task of cranking more laborious. Here too, despite some use of the crank for grinding, the labour involved was usually pointless. Another utterly pointless activity was shot drill, which consisted of lifting a 32-lb round shot, walking a few paces with it, and then repeating the process. Other, more rational, activities included sewing mailbags or making mats, while at the public works prisons work might include stone breaking, as at Portland and Dartmoor. In all prisons the 'house keeping' posts of cleaner or cooking assistant were eagerly competed for, and usually went to long-serving convicts with a sound good-conduct record.

Medical care was very rough-and-ready. Some doctors were more sympathetic than others, but all of them had to face their fair share of malingerers, feigners of madness, and self-inflicted wounds. On any given day 10 or 15 per cent of prisoners would see the doctor, and 100 examinations might be conducted in an hour. There would, therefore, be little agonizing over diagnosis and prescription, while, as even convict memoirs admitted, the proportion of malingerers was high. Unfortunately, this led many doctors, a number of whom would be very sceptical about prisoner ailments anyway, only to accept evidence of real illness when it was at an advanced stage. Indeed, release from prison on medical grounds was usually granted only to the terminally ill: the prison authorities would be unlikely to relish the thought of a coroner's inquest which would follow a fatality on the premises.

Discipline, too, was a snare which the prisoner had to confront. The idea of 'classes' or 'stages' in a prisoner's progress through his or her sentence meant that the most potent means of discipline in prison was usually the carrot: release might be quickened if the prisoner was industrious and well behaved. The major punishments for disciplinary offences within the prison were dietary punishment, solitary confinement, and flogging. The last, despite the emotive responses it aroused at the time and subsequently, was rarely used. Thus the Commissioners of Prisons *Report* for 1891 recorded that punishments inflicted on prisoners included the loss of stages and privileges to 9,793 male and 901 female prisoners; dietary punishments for 16,618 males and 1,652 females; punishment cells for 404 males and 167 females; iron handcuffs for 48 males and 98 females; and 107 cases of corporal punishment, all of them involving males.

In fact, the current secondary literature suggests that serious disciplinary problems were rare. There was, as there probably is in any prison system, a constant undertow of petty insubordination which, as the figures given above suggest, would result in a constant round of petty disciplinary proceedings. 'Breaking out', that is the destruction of a uniform or prison property, sometimes amounting to the smashing of a cell, occurred from time to time, but anything more serious was very uncommon. Certainly, there seems to have been little by way of large-scale insubordination or prison riots. The subject is, perhaps, one which requires further research, and there is certainly occasional evidence of larger tensions. There were early troubles in Millbank, in 1861 troops had to be brought in to restore order at Chatham, while in 1853–8 there were sit-down strikes, assaults on warders and escape attempts in the convict prisons by convicts angered at being denied transportation to Australia. But such incidents seem to have been far less common than they have become late in the twentieth century.

The problems of prison discipline introduces a related issue: the emergence of a professional prison staff.[24] As we have noted, from the outset one of the fundamentals of prison reform was the replacement of gaolers dependent upon fees by a salaried staff. The early nineteenth century saw a number of experiments, and the 1865 Prison Act formalized these by setting requirements for prison staff and making the important point that prisoners should not hold positions of responsibility. The Act envisaged a national establishment of 149 governors, 132 chaplains, 116 surgeons, 111 matrons, and about 3,700 subordinate posts. From the start, the English prison officer worked in a paramilitary system (indeed, many of the warders and most of the governors had a military background). At first, the uniformed staff carried out a number of tasks which have since been taken over by specialists: clerical, educational and instructional work, for example. As with the early police, attracting good recruits into the service and then keeping them there proved difficult. Thus it was found that in the 10 years before 1872, of 2,416 staff who had joined the service some 1,954 had left, and something of their quality can be gauged from the fact that in that year 417 disciplinary offences by staff were recorded in Millbank alone. A gradually burgeoning sense of solidarity among the warders, however, led in 1889 to a petition against low pay and bad working conditions. This petition, and the later deliberations of the Gladstone Committee, did little to bring real benefits, and a number of the problems that were to affect prison officers in the twentieth century were already present in 1900.

In this section we have devoted considerable space to the development of the prison system during the nineteenth century; justifiably so, given the significance of that process. Before moving on to other matters, it is necessary to restate briefly some of the salient themes. Perhaps the most important of these is to avoid any simplistic 'Whig interpretation' of prison history, from a barbaric eighteenth century to an enlightened Victorian era. Conditions in some eighteenth-century gaols were bad, but the penitentiary brought its own unpleasantnesses for the prisoner, and it is doubtful that the inmates of Clerkenwell house of correction who so disturbed Jacob Ilive would have regarded treading the wheel in one of Du Cane's local prisons as a release from barbarism. The change is not best interpreted as one involving differing degrees of humanity, but rather different degrees of regulation. The successful transition from a decentralized prison system administered locally to a uniformly administered national system must rank as one of the major domestic achievements of nineteenth-century central government. It should also be remembered that the activities of politicians and civil servants were carried out against the background of an informed public debate, in which the activities of proponents of reform, often well organized into pressure groups and lobbies, were vital. Even so, there was no unilinear progress: the most obvious sign of this was the changing emphasis over the century, at first on reforming the prisoner, then on simple punishment, and then, with the Gladstone Committee, a return to reform (and, as we shall see, the emergence of a number of other things) at the end of the century. If nothing else, however, the nineteenth-century prison system is worth the attention we have afforded it here because so much of it is still with us. It is almost a commonplace among both historians of the prison and penologists of the more modern system that a Victorian prisoner would find much that is familiar (including, in many cases, the actual structure) in a modern British gaol, while many of our assumptions and confusions about what prisons are for and what ought to be done in them were already current in the nineteenth century. These, too, are matters to which we shall return later.

The Wider Perspective

It is the prison, then, which has been seen as the major innovation in nineteenth-century punishment, and which Foucault, Ignatieff and others have seen as symbolizing the era's attitudes to punishment. Such opinions are understandable, and have much to recommend them. Yet it should be remembered that throughout the century the prison was only one aspect of the system of punishment. At one end of the spectrum older forms, notably the death penalty, were retained. At the other, a range of innovations were adopted, many of them aiming at a more humane treatment of offenders, many of them laying the foundations for developments with which we are now familiar. It is to these broader developments that we shall now turn.[25]

A strong case was made for the abolition of capital punishment throughout the second half of the nineteenth century. The case never got very far during that period, but the move towards a more restricted use of the death penalty over the early nineteenth century was very marked. It was the Offences Against the Person Act 1861 which finally abolished the death penalty for all offences other than murder and high treason, but in effect no executions other than for murder had taken place since the 1840s. By 1845–54 only 9 persons, all of them murderers, were hanged annually on average, compared to 66, of whom 13 were murderers, hanged annually between 1805 and 1814.[26] As the debates on abolition showed, however, one unresolved area was whether or not the existing methods of assessing culpability in homicide cases were sufficiently sophisticated. One area of innovation was in the treatment of insane offenders. Insanity had long been grounds for defence at English common law, but it seems to have been rarely invoked in the seventeenth or eighteenth centuries.[27] Following the acquittal of Daniel M'Naghten in 1843, however, rules intended for general application to criminal trials where insanity was pleaded were laid down. Whatever their imperfections, these rules were responsible for doubling the proportion of those being found insane in murder cases, from about 10 per cent of accused before 1843 to around 20 per cent in 1900. For the sane murderer, the royal prerogative of mercy continued to be regularly invoked, while it is possible that the continued presence of the death penalty was encouraging juries not to convict in the more uncertain murder cases. Thus by about 1900, 20 per cent of those accused of murder, as we have seen, would be found insane, another 40 per cent acquitted, and up to half of the remainder reprieved. Thus the death penalty's employment was becoming even more restricted, while it is interesting to note that the grounds upon which reprieves were granted would have been perfectly comprehensible in the early eighteenth century: absence of intent, the youth of the offender, and provocation, while many infanticides were acquitted.[28]

If capital punishment continued, so to did corporal punishment. By the mid nineteenth century it could be inflicted on four sets of offenders: adult offenders; juvenile offenders; incorrigible vagrants; and those committing serious infringements of prison regulations. Flogging was also, of course, part of the discipline of the armed forces, not being abolished in the army until 1881.[29] Despite its widespread use in the seventeenth and eighteenth centuries, whipping fell into disuse in the early nineteenth, and the abolition of flogging in public in 1862 could be interpreted as a sign of changing sensibilities. Flogging enjoyed a tremendous boost from the panic legislation which followed the garrotting scare of 1862, when a series of street robberies in the capital generated major social fear.[30]

This fuelled the desire for harshness against criminals which we have already noted in the early 1860s, and the subsequent Security from Violence Act introduced flogging as an additional punishment to penal servitude for robbery or attempted robbery with violence, or garrotting – that is choking, strangling, or suffocating in order to commit an offence. The judge could order a prisoner to have one, two or three bouts of flogging (25 strokes at a time for a person aged less than 16, with adults receiving 50 a time). This Act encouraged a number of other proposals to extend corporal punishment, most of which failed to make any progress.[31]

The motives behind the desire to flog were predictable, and most of the arguments involved still surface occasionally today. One of the major arguments in favour of corporal punishment was that it was speedy and inflicted physical pain. Even some humanitarians found the immediacy of flogging something which made it preferable to imprisonment in some cases, while non-humanitarians were likely to see the pain it inflicted as its greatest advantage. A second major argument in favour of flogging was that it humiliated the offender. The counter argument, that such degrading treatment might demoralize and harden the recipient, was often put forward by humanitarians. Thirdly, flogging was seen as an appropriate punishment for violent offenders. There was a strong element of retribution here, a feeling that like was being returned for like, while flogging also symbolized the revulsion which was felt against some offences. In the last resort, however, it seems that the most important reason for retaining or extending flogging as a punishment was that it provided enormous satisfaction to a frightened or vengeful public opinion. Certainly, as is so often the case in such circumstances, counter arguments based on rationality or statistics were brushed aside as irrelevant.[32]

Flogging also existed on the statute book as a punishment for incorrigible vagrants, but it was rarely invoked against them. Perhaps its most interesting use, however, was envisaged by the Vagrancy Act Amendment Act 1898, which extended previous legislation to cover those living on the immoral earnings of prostitutes. Yet even after this legislation flogging under the Vagrancy Acts was rare. There was one celebrated occasion when the chairman of the London sessions ordered thirty persons to be flogged during a drive against prostitution in 1912, but this was an isolated incident. In the early twentieth century no more than four floggings were ordered annually against indecent exposure – also within the ambit of vagrancy legislation – while the Home Office contacted magistrates deploring the practice when a few old men were flogged for sleeping rough.[33] Corporal punishment for juveniles was another matter, and was carried out throughout the nineteenth century, being regarded as a useful alternative to imprisonment for juvenile offenders. The levels of enforcement varied enormously, as did the age of offenders punished and the number of strokes given; and the punishment was sometimes carried out in the face of public hostility and the reluctance of the policemen who had to inflict it. Juveniles could be flogged for larceny, for malicious injury to property, under the garrotting legislation, and for the carnal knowledge of a girl aged under thirteen. The flogging of juveniles was rarely ordered by the assizes or quarter sessions, but was employed increasingly by the courts of summary jurisdiction. Some 590 juveniles were flogged on average annually between 1858 and 1860, a figure which rose to 2,900 in 1873 and 3,400 in 1900.[34] Corporal punishment for both adult and juvenile offenders was abolished in 1948.

The Victorians, to their credit, attempted to do more constructive things with young offenders than whip them, and their efforts in this direction involved some of the most innovatory aspects of nineteenth-century practices in the treatment of criminals. The concept of juvenile delinquency was essentially a Victorian invention,[35] connected not only to the wider context of ideas on social policy, but also to changing attitudes to childhood.[36] There had, of course, been earlier philanthropic schemes aimed at the young criminal, of which perhaps the most notable was the Marine Society founded in 1756, which aimed to send criminally inclined youths aged between 12 and 16 into the Royal Navy. Robert Young's Philanthropic Society, launched in 1788, was another noteworthy early experiment, while others occurred, often through the initiatives of local authorities or isolated philanthropists. By the early nineteenth century there was a growing feeling that young offenders, whether being transported or imprisoned, ought to be separated from adult criminals and treated differently from them. The fear of contamination, and the concomitant hope that the young offender, if caught early enough, might be saved from a life of crime and recidivism, was one of the most consistent themes in the period's insistence on the classification of convicted criminals.

This feeling, and a growing dissatisfaction with the existing practices for dealing with young offenders, led in 1835 to a governmental decision to establish a penitentiary for them. A disused barracks at Parkhurst on the Isle of Wight was chosen as the location, and its regimen set up by an Act of 1853. A stern discipline was envisaged, and the boys were to be trained to make them efficient labourers in the colonies where they were to be sent at the end of their detention. As with other penitentiaries, however, early notions of reforming inmates faded away, and after a decision to send younger (and hence more hopeful) cases on to the Philanthropic Society's school in Redhill, Parkhurst simply became a prison for young offenders. It was thought to be failing in its original objectives, and in 1864 was converted to a female convict establishment. This experiment was, therefore, a failure: yet the idea that it was desirable to offer special treatment to juvenile offenders survived. British supporters of this notion took a great interest in the agricultural reform schools, refuges and colonies which were being developed for young offenders in Belgium, France, Germany and the Netherlands. The Philanthropic Society's school at Redhill, which had been founded in 1849, was set up with these continental examples very much in mind. At about the same time one of that breed of redoubtable social reformers which the Victorian era threw up, Mary Carpenter, was popularizing the idea of a Reformatory Movement. Her arguments, founded on a deep religious conviction and a desire to save children from vice, struck a responsive chord in the early Victorian consciousness.

This burgeoning public concern was mirrored by governmental action. In 1847 a House of Lords Select Committee was set up to consider the treatment of juvenile offenders. There were, of course, objections to the very notion of 'treatment', and arguments on the familiar theme of less eligibility were trotted out. Thus Lord Denman deplored the idea that young offenders should be given 'benefits and privileges which they could never have hoped for but from the commission of crimes', and declared that he was 'extremely jealous of the gratuitous instruction of a young felon in a trade, merely because he is a felon'.[37] There was also a considerable lack of unity of purpose among the various strands of the reformatory movement. Nevertheless, a system of reformatory schools was established by parliamentary legislation, with the Reformatory Schools Act of 1854 being followed by the Industrial Schools Act of 1857. In 1866 a consolidating and amending Act laid the basis for the reformatory and industrial schools for the next quarter century. By that date there were about 50 reformatory schools, while there were 99 industrial schools by 1884, and the population of the industrial schools was to reach 24,500 by 1893. Of those sent to the reformatory schools, about 80 per cent were charged with simple larceny, and between a third and a half were first offenders. The way forward for the creation of further institutions was cleared by the Education Act of 1876, and by 1914 there were 43 reformatories, 132 industrial schools, 21 day industrial schools and 12 truant schools. As much as the adult prison system, the erection of these institutions represented a formidable ideological and material commitment to penal policy. The state was now making a massive incursion into society in an attempt to do something about the stratum of vagrant and pauper children which contemporary opinion regarded as the core of the criminal class of the next generation.

Yet once again the ideal of being able to reform and save offenders faded. The reformatories were too much like prisons to be able to do much by way of reform. In the reformatory the inmate's day lasted from 6 a.m. to 8 or 9 p.m., with eight hours of hard work, and comparatively little by way of education. Discipline was enforced by fines or withdrawal of privileges, although the birch was occasionally employed as a tougher sanction. Food was sparse, silence was enforced at mealtimes, and clothing was plain and coarse. The idea of less eligibility was firmly entrenched, and so the small amount of education and training offered was justified by its implementors as not putting inmates at any advantage when they re-entered the outside world; and prison staff were usually insufficiently trained or qualified to carry out these aspects of their duties anyway.

By 1914 a number of concerns over the deficiencies of the reformatories were being voiced. Indeed, as early as 1900, 'the heyday of the institution as the solution to the problem of juvenile delinquency was over'.[38]

Indeed, shortly after that point a new departure in the treatment of young offenders was heralded by the introduction of the probation system. Ultimately the origins of probation might be traced back to the practice, already existing in the seventeenth century, of putting suspected offenders under recognizance to keep the peace or be of good behaviour rather than punishing them, a practice which by the early nineteenth century was being employed regularly as an alternative to short terms of imprisonment. The real impetus, however, came from Massachusetts, where in 1869 the 'State Agents' had set up a system, within which the basics of the modern notion of probation were established, for monitoring young offenders. The system caught the attention of British observers, and in 1886 the Probation of First Offenders Act was passed. Initially little use was made of the provisions of the Act, but the system was overhauled and in 1907 was set on a firmer basis by a Liberal government bent on social reform. The Act was followed by various government publications and directives, the net result of which was that by the outbreak of the First World War social work was firmly embedded in the system of criminal justice. The offender was to be supervised by carefully chosen professionals, and the object of the system was to ensure that offenders reformed themselves with the advice and the assistance of the probation officer. This added a new dimension to crime control, and demonstrated further the state's willingness to extend its activities and powers over the criminal.[39]

Attention was also turned to new ways of dealing with adult offenders. It is one of the great ironies of the nineteenth century that, having established the prison as the standard means of punishing crime, ever increasing attention was paid to finding alternatives to sending offenders to prison. One of the unexpected results of the extension of imprisonment was the production of a group of constant recidivists. Such people had doubtlessly existed before the nineteenth century, but the arrival of a more bureaucratic punishment system meant that their activities were better recorded, as was the catalogue of penalties imposed upon them. One such was Samuel Taverner, a labourer born about 1839, whose dismal criminal career was charted in the records of the Bedfordshire quarter sessions. In 1855 he received his first sentence, three months in gaol for stealing fowls. He was charged on fifteen subsequent occasions for stealing, assault, wilful damage, offences against the game laws, being drunk and riotous, and being a suspicious person. Most of his sentences were short: six weeks for wilful damage in 1857, a month for assault in 1858, a month for stealing cabbages in 1865. He received three years' penal servitude for stealing manure bags in 1862, but apparently offended shortly after his release. In 1867 he was given seven years' penal servitude for stealing goods to the value of 3s. Once again, he apparently re-offended shortly after release at the end of this sentence, and in 1874 made his seventeenth appearance before the courts, this time for stealing cloth to the value of £1, and was sentenced to ten years of penal servitude to be followed by seven years of police supervision.[40] Whatever else the Victorian penal system was achieving, it was manifestly neither deterring nor reforming Samuel Taverner.

The obvious point arising from such careers is that most prison sentences were short. The work of Foucault and Ignatieff has obscured the point that, whatever was going on at Pentonville or other penitentiaries, most offenders entering English gaols in the nineteenth century were not there long enough for the state to get to work on their souls, or for reformation to be imposed upon them. Taking the findings of one excellent local study, we discover that between 1835 and 1860 some 11,529 sentences were imposed for larceny in the Black Country. Of these 17 per cent were of imprisonment for less than a month, 42.8 per cent for between one and three months, 19.1 per cent for between four and six months, and 6.4 per cent for between seven and twelve months. Leaving aside the 8.6 per cent involving transportation and the 2.2 per cent involving penal servitude, it is obvious that most petty thieves received only a very short spell in prison; much the same was true of sentences for receiving stolen goods, embezzlement, and fraud.[41]

For an impression of the inmates in a local gaol at a later period let us turn to a sample of nearly 3,600 prisoners who passed through Wakefield gaol in a three month period in 1877. Three quarters of them were male, about half of them came from the West Riding, with most of the remainder, 602 Irish apart, coming from other parts of England. Over a third were convicted for drunkenness, and many of the others were petty offenders: rogues and vagabonds, vagrants, disorderly paupers, and common prostitutes. More serious offenders were represented by the 489 convicted for felony, and the 426 convicted for assault or aggravated assault. About a third of them were illiterate, and only 31 (there was one other described as 'superior' in educational attainment) could write well. There was a wide age range, although the biggest groups were the 1,204 prisoners in their twenties and the 974 in their thirties. Those who had been committed to prison before numbered 1,909, of whom 287 had been imprisoned more than ten times. Total committals to Wakefield Gaol for the year ending 30 September 1877 were 12,504: the average daily population of the prison over these twelve months was 1,401.6, suggesting that the bulk of those committed, as in the earlier Black Country sample, were only experiencing a month or two's imprisonment.[42]

It is evident, therefore, that large numbers of people were experiencing imprisonment in this period, and that for some of them it was a repeated experience. Yet there remained a number of alternative punishments at the disposal of the magistrates. By the early twentieth century these could range from fines or discharge with or without sureties to discharge under a probation officer or short term detention in a special institution. The range of punishments was applied to a larger number of offenders as criminal business began to move away from the assizes and quarter sessions to the summary jurisdiction of magistrates. Legislation (notably an Act of 1855 empowering magistrates to try larcenies up to the value of 5s., and another of 1879 which allowed them to try indictable offences committed by children aged under twelve) extended the magistrates' powers of summary jurisdiction, and the growth in their business is striking. In 1854 21,000 offenders in England and Wales were tried at the assizes and quarter sessions for indictable offences and 3,000 before the magistrates: by 1881 the respective figures were 10,000 and 46,000. This shift was accompanied by some important changes in the punishments inflicted. In 1836, of each 1,000 offenders sentenced at higher and summary courts for indictable offences, 33 were sentenced to death, 245 to transportation or penal servitude, 685 to imprisonment, and 21 to a fine. By

1912, those sentenced to death numbered 0.4 per 1,000 with 15 receiving penal servitude, 390 being imprisoned, 173 being fined, 12 placed on probation following conviction, and 304, after the charge against them being proved, receiving an order made without conviction that they should undergo probation or related measures.[43]

The nineteenth century may have been the century of the prison, but it is noteworthy that by its end the willingness to send many categories of offender to prison was much abated. It is worth pondering how far this return to greater flexibility, which demonstrated that the penal mood was moving away from incarceration, may have been in a certain sense a parallel of pre-prison practices. Petty sessions have not been much studied for the earlier period and obviously a number of sentencing options open to the magistrates in 1900 were simply not available in the seventeenth or eighteenth centuries. Then, too, however – albeit within a more limited range of options – sentencing on summary conviction was undoubtedly marked by a flexible approach, probably involving considerable use of small fines, informal orders of restitution, and binding over to keep the peace or to be of good behaviour.

A more basic contribution towards keeping people out of prison was (and is) giving offenders leaving prison the assistance which would help them in beginning a new and non-criminal life. As we have noted, many individuals involved in the early prison reform movement were impelled by philanthropic motives, and from the outset the need to do something to aid discharged prisoners was identified as an urgent priority. Some provisions for this were envisaged in the Gaol Act of 1823, and local or individual initiatives were encouraged further by an Act of 1862 which attempted to standardize procedures, this tendency being encouraged by further legislation in 1877. All these measures applied only to local prisons; those who emerged after serving their time in a convict prison were discharged on ticket of leave and subjected to a period of police supervision. But after 1860 they too could benefit from the Discharged Prisoners' Aid Society (soon to become a Royal Society) set up by Samuel Whitbread.

These developments were, however, only partially successful. Any proposals to implement a full scale aftercare service were predictably denounced as 'ultra-philanthropy', and there was little agreement as to which prisoners should be assisted, or about the nature or extent of the assistance which should be offered to them. The greatest impediment to assistance, however, was the sheer size of the problem. By the late nineteenth century 3,000 convicts and 100,000 local prisoners were being released annually, far too many to be given meaningful assistance with the existing resources. Yet these early efforts, however insufficient, and however flavoured by Victorian perceptions about deserving objects of charity, were at least an attempt to grapple with that most difficult problem, the reintegration of the offender into society.[44]

As we have noted, the Gladstone Committee's Report of 1895 ushered in an age of optimism in penal affairs. To some extent this optimism was fuelled by the marked fall in prison population over the later nineteenth century. In 1877–8 the average daily population of convicts was 10,139, and of local prisoners 20,833. In 1893–4 the totals had fallen to 4,383 and 13,850 respectively, a fall especially encouraging during a period of general population increase. As the Committee remarked, too simplistic a reading of these figures was to be avoided: yet it also pointed to the fact that the fall in the prison population could be set against a slight fall, from 217 per 100,000 of the population in 1874–8 to 194 in 1889–93, in the number of indictable offences tried at the assizes, quarter sessions, and courts of summary conviction (*Report from the Departmental Committee on Prisons*, 1895, p. 3). Modern research has suggested that this falling crime rate was due to a whole complex of factors, of which relative economic prosperity was probably the most important, but in which the influence of penal institutions was at best uncertain:[45] yet it is difficult to blame late Victorian and Edwardian observers for deriving considerable satisfaction from these figures, and for attributing them in large measure to the system of punishments that was in operation.

This point reintroduces the problem of the wider significance of the rise of the prison as the main, and indeed symbolic, form of punishment in the nineteenth century. As we have seen, a number of writers have attempted to attach a very deep significance to the prison, whether this lies in the straightforward connection between the rise of industrial capitalism, the factory, and the penitentiary prison, or the more recent, and more complex, theories of Foucault. The products of such writers are, of course, very welcome, in that they are powerful stimulants to reaching a deeper level of theorizing than that normally accomplished by the mainstream of British historians. They do however tend to suffer some hard knocks when their theories are set against what empirical research can reconstruct of the reality of nineteenth-century prison life.

The gulf between theory and practice is demonstrated neatly by Margaret de Lacy, who, after discussing the attention lavished upon Bentham's Panopticon by Foucault and others, comments that 'whatever the Panopticon represents, English society baulked at adopting it'.[46] The history of the prison, like the history of most things, alters radically when we turn from the projects of great thinkers to the rather more messy context of reality.

Conversely, Foucault's work has come near to establishing itself as the standard interpretation of the meaning of the prison in western culture: as one recent critic has written, it has 'an out-of-the-ordinariness which never fails to provide comment and discussion and . . . a kind of intellectual charisma which attaches to the book and its author'.[47] Perhaps for our immediate purposes, the most important issue is not whether Foucault's views on the prison are correct, but rather to grasp the underlying importance of his formulation of the changes in the way in which power, and in particular the power to punish criminals, is expressed. Foucault, it will be remembered, claimed that there was a shift, centred on the period 1780–1820, from punishments aimed at the bodies of offenders to punishments directed at their souls. This shift itself was part of a wider process in which control over offenders (and society in general) passed increasingly into the hands of 'experts'. Physical force, and punitive public ceremonies, were replaced by a type of power based on a bureaucratic knowledge of offenders, routine intervention, and a gentler corrective style.

Obviously, there is much in Foucault's arguments: the rise of the prison can be interpreted as one facet of much wider alterations in the way in which government interacts with society. And, more importantly, as we shall argue in the next chapter, the involvement of what might be termed 'technicians' has become central to the way in which twentieth-century Britain treats its criminals.

A number of problems remain, however. Foucault, like so many writers, tended to flatten pre-1750 developments, to overrate the barbarity, and to underrate the major shifts in the two centuries preceding that date. More immediately, empirical research on prison conditions, especially local prison conditions, has indicated that the actuality of prison life was, as de Lacy has argued so strongly, considerably less tidy than any of the grand theorists have suggested. Moreover, the idea of a transition from punishment directed at the body to punishment directed at the soul is less clear-cut than Foucault suggests: prisoners in the hulks in the 1820s, or sleeping on planks, eating a prison diet, and treading the wheel in the 1870s might have thought that the experience of incarceration was aimed at their physical comfort as much as that of their minds. The variety of punishments available also causes some problems: it is difficult to fit transportation or the continued widespread use of fining into Foucault's scheme. Any idea of an easy connection between the prison and the rise of industrial capitalist society is also a little difficult to sustain on a simple level. Of the early proponents of new model prisons, the Duke of Richmond, Sir George Onesiphorus Paul, and John Howard himself make poor representatives of industrial capitalism, while de Lacy has argued that in industrialized Lancashire it was the gentry who were the pacemakers of penal reform: the main concern of the industrialists was to keep costs down. And, of course, we must reiterate the great irony. Capital punishment, it has been claimed, was symbolic of pre-industrial judicial punishment, replaced by the prison in the nineteenth century, but just as the period of the ascendancy of capital punishment was marked by the courts trying to find ways of allowing criminals to escape the noose, so the nineteenth century saw the beginnings of what was to become a continuing process of keeping some offenders (most notably young offenders) who were thought worthy, from incarceration. Yet, like the smile on the Cheshire Cat, Pentonville, Dartmoor, Parkhurst and the rest remain. These edifices are one of the major legacies which the Victorian era has left us: so are some of the attitudes about punishment which underpinned them.

IV

The Twentieth Century

England and Wales entered the twentieth century with a system of judicial punishments which showed, in embryo at least, a number of differing trends. At the centre of the system, practically and symbolically, stood the prison. Hardly thought of as a dominant form of punishment for the serious offender in 1800, by 1900 the prison was firmly established in both the popular consciousness and the practice of the courts as the most potent means by which the generality of offenders might be punished.

After 1877 the prison system was under tight control from central government. Around the prison, there were the first vestiges of that range of institutions, pressure groups and experts which are so familiar a part of the way in which we currently treat criminals. Many would see these as representing a softer line on criminals, others would see them as representing wider, more subtle, and ultimately more effective means of controlling criminals than straightforward repression. In a curious sense, the modern probation officer is fulfilling the same function as did the regular reprieving of capitally convicted adolescents in the eighteenth century.

An historical training inhibits the historian from approaching the past with the present too overtly in mind; yet, for the late twentieth-century Briton, the contrast between our current situation and that obtaining early this century is so striking as to make avoiding comment impossible. As we drift from expedient to expedient in the face of rising crime figures and rising levels of empty governmental rhetoric about law and order, it is fascinating to look back to a period when informed opinion thought that crime was lessening, that the established penal system was fundamentally sound, but that

that system could be rendered even better by constructive and forward-looking improvements.

An Age of Optimism

The tone of early twentieth-century penal policy was set by the Prison Act of 1898. Broadly, it was this Act which made possible the 'penal-welfare complex' which was largely constructed over the early years of this century and which is still with us.[1] More narrowly, the possibilities for an amelioration of the regimes in convict prisons were opened up by the premise that the way in which sentences of penal servitude and imprisonment were carried out could be regulated by rules made by the Home Secretary. These were to be placed before parliament, and became statutory unless objected to inside a period of thirty days.

This new power was used to modify a number of aspects of the existing prison regime. In particular, the full power of separate confinement was diluted, while the older forms of hard labour were abolished and the philosophy which underlay them replaced with the notion that prison labour should be productive and should, as the 1899 prison rules put it, if practicable, 'be such as will fit the prisoner to earn his livelihood on release'. In line with this latter provision, the treadwheel and the crank were abolished (interestingly, shot drill had already been abolished by Du Cane). Further reforms were enacted in the treatment of the medically defective and the unstable, in the medical care of prisoners, and in provisions for prisoners after discharge. The mood of optimism is, perhaps, most notably enshrined (again in the wording of the 1899 rules) in the attitudes recommended to prison officers:

> It is the duty of all officers to treat prisoners with kindness and humanity . . . the great object of reclaiming the criminal should always be kept in view by all officers, and they should strive to acquire a moral influence over the prisoners by performing their duties conscientiously, but without harshness.

That such a state of affairs proved unattainable should not surprise us; that it was regarded as feasible is a striking testimony to the spirit of the age.

The period was also marked by the influence of two major reformers. The first of these, Sir Evelyn Ruggles-Brise, was born into an Essex gentry family in 1857. After attending Eton and Balliol, he entered the Home Office in 1881, served as a private secretary to five successive Home Secretaries, and in 1895 was promoted to Chairman of the Prison Commission, a post he held until his retirement in 1921 (he died in 1935). Ruggles-Brise acquired his chairmanship in the aftermath of the Gladstone Committee Report, and in the mood of the times used the 1898 Prison Act to obtain a more liberal regime in prisons. It was under his chairmanship that the borstal system originated and that the important Crime Act of 1908 entered the statute book.[2] The second major figure was Sir Alexander Paterson, born in Cheshire, the son of a solicitor, in 1884. His family was involved in good works locally, and while at Oxford Paterson took up voluntary social work and spent the next twenty years continuing these activities in Bermondsey. His work there included the care of borstal boys and discharged prisoners, and after war service (he was awarded the MC and wounded) he became a member of the prison commission in 1922. A devoutly religious man, Paterson saw his work as a prison administrator to be a struggle against the mental and moral deterioration which prison caused its inmates. He was tremendously energetic, spent a large amount of time visiting prisons and borstals, studied foreign prisons at first hand and was very influential. The idealism and energy of Paterson and his associates, viewed from the perspective of the late twentieth century, looks like evidence of a lost Golden Age of penal policy.[3]

An optimistic attitude towards matters penal was aided in the early twentieth century by a continuation of that downward trend in imprisonment which we have seen in the late Victorian period. In 1921, Hobhouse and Brockway stated confidently in their survey of the prison system that 'it is good to be able to say at the outset that our prison population is strongly diminished'. The figures they cited supported this contention: the average daily population in the local prisons was about 20,000 in 1876–7, 14,300 in 1913–14, and 8,400 in 1921. The equivalent figures for convict prisons were 10,000, 2,700 and 1,400. 'The prison population last year,' they concluded, 'was, therefore, considerably less than one-third of what it was 40 years ago.' Other figures they cited, including those involving admissions into prison and the ratio of prisoners per 100,000 of the population demonstrated this trend in other ways. Moreover at the time they wrote most people going to prison were still serving only very short sentences. The average length of time served in a local prison was five weeks, in a convict prison four years and ten weeks. Of the 48,588 prisoners sent to local prisons in 1920–1, 11,950 were sentenced to two weeks or less.[4]

These statistical grounds for optimism were to continue into the immediate post-Second World War period. The Commissioners' Report for 1947, which took the story to the year ending 31 December 1946, showed a total of receptions of roughly the same order (about 30,000) as that obtaining in the average annual total for the five years ended 31 December 1940. This in turn contrasted with an average annual total of receptions for the five years ended 31 December 1931 of 41,063, and 37,548 for the five years ended 31 December 1935. These reports were constantly looking back to the high levels of imprisonment obtaining in the Victorian and pre-First World War eras. Thus in 1951 the Commissioners' report contrasted the 29,835 male and 2,986 female receptions for 1950 with the 105,510 male and 33,733 female in 1913. These figures do not, however, indicate as clear-cut a situation as might at first seem. A high proportion of receptions in the pre-First World War period were people unable to pay small fines, mostly for drunkenness. Legislation of 1914 which enabled such people to be given time to pay their fines rather than imprisoning them if they could not pay immediately led to a rapid and marked diminution in the levels of reception into prisons. Yet it is noteworthy that even in the 1930s the majority of prison sentences were still for very short periods. In 1938, 51.0 per cent of male and 70.7 per cent of female prisoners were serving sentences of less than a month, and 23.9 per cent of male and 15.3 per cent of female for more than one month but less than three. Only 116 men and 1 woman were sentenced for over five years.

Despite the fall in the number of prisoners, the costs of imprisonment had increased. In 1881 the gross cost of the prison system was (to the nearest pound) £361,130, and the net cost (the difference being largely accounted for by the value of convict labour)

£147,046, which meant that the annual average cost of keeping a prisoner was just over £14. Of the gross cost, staff wages and allowances were £171,076, staff uniforms £5,266, food for prisoners £94,638, clothing for prisoners £27,252, and fuel and light for prisons £21,244. By 1938 the costs of running the system had risen to £1,763,981 gross, or £1,483,191 net, giving an annual cost per prisoner of about £131. Staff salaries, at £742,827, were still the largest single item, while interestingly the overall cost of feeding the prison population had barely risen, standing at £105,043. The cost of clothing, bedding and furniture for prisoners now stood at £56,977, and fuel, light, etc. at £106,897. Medical expenses for prisoners had risen to £4,837, compared to £2,293 in 1881. The net costs of the prison service had risen, in money terms, tenfold between 1881 and 1938.[5]

Part of the reason for these increased costs was the more varied nature of the institutions grouped within the prison system. Perhaps the most interesting of these was the open prison. In some respects a contradiction in terms, the open prison marked (and still marks) a move away from the fundamental supposition that the main role of imprisonment is simply containment. The open prison is a testimony to the continued faith in the reformatory potential of punishment, and as such is under constant pressure both from public opinion and politicians pandering to it. The first open prison, which still in fact had some closed sections, was founded in 1891 at Witzwil, Switzerland, the creation of the penal reformer Otto Kellerhals. Experiments also took place in the United States. In 1916 the Lorton Reformatory, which had no containing walls, was founded, and by the late 1930s the United States could boast such well known open institutions as the Californian Institution for men at Chino, Southern California, and the federal open prison at Seagoville, Texas. In Britain, the first open prison was located at New Hall Camp, a satellite of Wakefield Prison, in 1933. Doubts about the whole concept were to some extent allayed by the fact that only seven prisoners absconded during the first fifteen years of the institution's life. By 1975 there were thirteen open prisons with an average daily population of 3,230.[6]

The philosophy behind the open prison was very aptly summed up by one of Paterson's most quoted maxims: 'You cannot train a man for freedom under conditions of captivity.' Thus the open prison represented yet another aspect of the reformatory ideal, with its assumption that it was indeed possible to 'train a man (and later, a woman) for freedom'. The proponents of the scheme saw it as an especially handy means of combating 'prisonization', a term first made accessible by one of the earliest serious sociological studies of prison life, Donald Clemmer's *The Prison Community* of 1940. Clemmer, basing his researches on a maximum security prison in Illinois, found that the standard policy of containment led to the institutionalization and prisonization of inmates. While the inmate culture reinforced their criminality, the process of institutionalization posed a more insidious threat by making the inmates increasingly incapable of taking those decisions and initiatives which are part of everyday life: one of the things prison does, to some of those passing through it, is make them increasingly unable to function independently. To counter this, as Kenyon Scudder, the Warden of Chino, put it, the open prison aims to 'challenge each individual to stand on his own feet',[7] and thus encourage inmates to be social rather than anti-social beings. The optimism behind the open prison had to be backed up with resources and with the encouragement of more flexible attitudes among prison officers. In time, what was regarded by many as a dubious experiment in the 1930s has now become a viable and accepted part of the British penal system, although it should be noted that part of its success is due to the peculiar nature of its inmates. Those incarcerated in open prisons tend to be white-collar or similar criminals, many of them of a middle-class background.

Another major innovation, this time having its origins back in the Gladstone Report, was the borstal system.[8] The Committee envisaged special treatment for adolescent offenders aged between sixteen and twenty-one, foreseeing some type of reformatory for offenders in this age group which should be a half-way house between the prison and the reformatory. This should combine education and training with a penal and coercive aspect, and should, ideally, be located in the countryside. The Committee was rightly concerned about the number of young offenders, and felt that the habitual offenders of the future might be eliminated if criminal instincts could be nipped in the bud during adolescence. In a certain sense, therefore, the origins of the borstal system lay in its being yet another attempt at solving what had long been regarded as a central problem, that of catching young offenders before they became hardened criminals. As with the reformatory movement, the immediate inspiration came from abroad. The Gladstone Committee was particularly impressed by reports of the reformatory at Elmira in New York State, which claimed that 80 per cent of those passing through it never re-offended. Ruggles-Brise went over to examine the methods used at Elmira, and his subsequent report, while not wholly uncritical of some of the practices used there, recognized the basic ideas as sound ones. After some debate, the new experiment in the treatment of young offenders began when six young prisoners were transferred from various London prisons to Bedford Prison. In 1901 part of the convict prison at Borstal was converted for the keeping of young offenders: 'it is significant', wrote one of the subsequent students of the borstal system, 'that the first party arrived in chains'.[9]

The borstal system initially envisaged the strict classification of inmates, firm discipline, hard work and organized supervision on discharge. So attractive did the idea seem that it spread through much of the prison system, until by 1922, a 'modified borstal system' was applied to all offenders aged between sixteen and twenty-one, even those only sentenced for a short term. With the Prevention of Crime Act 1908 the term 'borstal institution' entered the language of crime and punishment. It was now accepted that the assizes and quarter sessions, when sentencing persons in the appropriate age range, might send those who might be felt to benefit from the regime to a borstal institution for between one and three years. The system at first expanded fairly slowly, a second institution, Feltham, being opened in 1911, and a third, Portland, in 1921. The arrival of Alexander Paterson as commissioner in charge of borstals put a new force into the borstal idea, and from the mid 1930s onwards borstals were regarded as an accepted, and generally praiseworthy, part of the wider penal system. The Report of the Departmental Committee on the Treatment of Young Offenders of 1927 encouraged extending the system further, and by the 1930s the borstal was widely accepted as the appropriate punishment for young offenders. A number of new borstal institutions were opened, notably at Camp Hill in 1931 and Bagthorpe in 1932, while the general confidence in the system can be gauged by the setting up of Lowdham Grange open borstal in 1931.

All this did not take place without considerable public debate and some opposition. It was widely believed that, despite the intentions behind them, borstals were seminaries for future criminals, while the less-eligibility argument was, as ever when anything constructive about dealing with offenders is suggested, used frequently. It appeared during the initial debates on the Elmira reformatory, and as late as 1932 it was possible for the *Sunday Pictorial* to deplore the way borstal boys were 'made adoptive sons of the state . . . and generally mollycoddled through life by fussy sentimentalists at the public expense'.[10] In fact, from the beginning borstals aimed at a strict regime. Discipline in general was tight and the stress laid on the earning of privileges through good conduct, together with the emphasis on gymnastics and early rising, reflected the contemporary notion that the offender was in need of physical as well as moral regeneration. Work was also seen as an essential part of the borstal system. It was usually justified on the grounds that it would fit the offender for employment on returning to the outside world, although it became obvious that what borstals did was discipline adolescents into the work ethic rather than teach them a trade as such. Additionally, there is a distinct impression that the overall effect of borstal was to mix the ethos of the prison with that of the public school. This point was neatly illustrated by Paterson, who in 1925 remarked that

> borstal training is based on the double assumption that there is individual good in each, and among nearly all an innate corporate spirit which will respond to the appeal made to the British of every sort to play the game, follow the flag, to stand by the old ship.[11]

The subsequent introduction of the house system furnishes further evidence of the public school model. The objective of all this was to inculcate working-class youth with middle-class values. But, if we may quote Roger Hood again, 'the inmates were not, however, asked to become middle class themselves; they were expected to fulfil the bourgeois image of the "honest workman" '.[12] Thus even borstal, for all the undoubted idealism of many of those involved in running the system, was clearly, in the last resort, different from the prison only in that it offered a subtler means of expressing power and controlling. Yet by the 1930s borstal could be portrayed as a success: to take a typical sample, of those released from borstal in 1936, only 30 per cent had been reconvicted within two years.

A less happy invention, in this case a direct product of the Prevention of Crime Act 1908, was preventive detention, conceived as a method of dealing with that other long-standing object of concern, the recidivist. Preventive detention permitted the court to award two sentences to the habitual offender, one for the actual offence being tried, and one for being a recidivist. A preventive detention prison was set up at Camp Hill on the Isle of Wight, adjacent to Parkhurst. The regime of preventive detention was a relatively light one, certainly less onerous than penal detention and, as described by Hobhouse and Brockway, offered a flexible and humane method of dealing with recidivists. The system was, however, little used. During 1912–13 out of 871 persons sentenced to penal servitude only 85 were sentenced to penal detention, and only 44 out of 482 in 1920–1. In 1913–14 the average daily population in penal detention was only 171, and this had sunk to 31 by 1947. The reason for this disinclination to use penal detention was, according to Howard Jones, that 'it was not in accordance with the tradition of just retribution which dominates judicial thinking in this country, to impose two penalties for one crime, and on the whole the courts were not prepared to do it'.[13] A more practical consideration, perhaps, was a feeling that the recidivists who might have been sent to Camp Hill were too late in their careers to be affected by preventive detention. Even so, early statistics showed that the reconviction rate of those who had undergone preventive detention was gratifyingly low.

The years between the Gladstone Committee Report and the First World War saw the flowering of notions of 'treating' criminals, the meshing of such notions with broader ideas on social policy, and the emergence of what has been described as a 'penal-welfare complex'.[14] Nowhere is this point demonstrated more clearly than the development of the probation service. By 1912, we must reiterate, nearly a third of those sentenced for an indictable offence at a higher or summary court were being treated through probation and related measures.[15] The integration of the probation service into the system which Edwardian legislation had envisaged was confirmed by the Criminal Justice (Administration) Act 1914, and by 1922 the Departmental Committee on the Training, Appointment and Pay of Probation Officers clearly saw itself as being in control of a complex and fully professional system. The duties and powers of the probation service were extended further through the 1920s and 1930s. By the end of the latter decade this extension, notably into matrimonial disputes, meant that probation officers were virtually the social workers of the courts.[16]

One element in the penal system who were less than delighted with the innovatory and reformatory ethos of the Paterson era were the prison officers.[17] The easing of the separate system after 1895 meant that the prison staff had to move away from a practice based on straightforward coercion to the rather different techniques needed to keep associated prisoners under control. Obviously, punishment was still needed for infringements of prison regulations or more general acts of insubordination. Under normal conditions, however, the great aid to control, as had increasingly been the case in the nineteenth century, was the promise of privilege or the threat of withdrawing it. Well-behaved prisoners could earn privileges which made sentences shorter or life within the prison more tolerable, whilst the presence of such privileges gave the staff a means of control through the possibilities of removing them. Remission, whereby part of a sentence is dropped in return for the prisoner's good behaviour, has proved especially useful in this respect. Unfortunately, however, in the face of a more lenient regime with its greater emphasis on treatment, many officers (the title of warder was dropped along with the prison crop and the broad-arrow uniform in the 1920s) felt that their own position and problems were being neglected as the prisoners seemed to gain ever increasing attention. The officers were tightly disciplined, could still be fined for disciplinary failings, often lived in unsatisfactory quarters, and felt that their pay and conditions left them with much to complain about. This led to attempts at unionization. There had been rumblings among officers on the need for some sort of collective representation in the 1890s, and a more solid demand for a union arose in 1906, the idea being bitterly opposed by the incoming Home Secretary, Winston Churchill. In 1910 the founding of the *Prison Officers' Magazine* provided an organ for staff discontent. Some officers joined the National Union of Police and Prison Officers, and were involved in (and some of them dismissed after) that organization's strike of 1919. More long term survival was enjoyed by the Prison Officers' Representative Board, set up by the government as the official organ of communication between the officers and the prison commissioners, and hence immediately suspect to many of the uniformed staff. Finally, in 1938, the prison staff were allowed to form the Prison Officers' Association (POA).

The 1930s, indeed, witnessed a continuation of the worries and grievances of the uniformed staff. The reforms and reforming attitudes of the Paterson regime gained little by way of an enthusiastic response from the prison officers. They felt that their interests were being ignored, that the reforms were being carried through without their being consulted, and were in any case in an anomalous situation, caught as they were between the established ethos of containment and the revived mood of reformation and rehabilitation. A more consistent worry was generated by the way in which the needs of an ever more complex system meant that outsiders (in effect, Foucault's 'technicians') were increasingly being recruited into the system to perform specialist functions within the service. One result of this was that career opportunities were gradually blocked for the uniformed staff, who were being increasingly associated with that coercive aspect of prison work which the current penal philosophy seemed to be downgrading. Despite the appreciation of their work regularly expressed in the Prison Commissioners' annual reports, it was obvious that the uniformed staff were becoming alienated from the officially defined objectives of the prison service.

Despite the worries about controlling associated prisoners sometimes expressed by prison officers, serious problems in prisons seem to have been rare, although, as for the nineteenth century, the topic is seriously under-researched. There were occasional assaults upon officers, but figures published in 1923 showed that prison officers were less likely to suffer fatal or serious injury in the course of their duties than were railwaymen, and that they were only marginally more likely to do so than employees in factories and workshops.[18] There were isolated large-scale incidents, as in 1905 when troops had to be brought in to quell trouble at Maidstone, and there was rioting and an escape at Gloucester. By far the most serious incident of the first half of the twentieth century, however, came in January 1932 at Dartmoor. A period of mounting tension was brought to a head when prisoners complained about the quality of their porridge, a full-scale riot breaking out a few days later when the men were paraded before chapel. The prisoners took control of the gaol for a few hours, but were eventually contained with the help of the police and deterred from further trouble by the use of firearms. The subsequent inquiry showed little inclination to probe very much into the incident's deeper causes.[19] A recent historian of the prison officer, however, has put the Dartmoor incident within the context of the problems caused by the liberalization of the prison regime. In particular, it showed how the abolition of the separate system implied readjustments in the techniques of controlling prisoners.[20]

The attitudes of the first half of the twentieth century were summed up in the Criminal Justice Act 1948. This began by abolishing penal servitude, hard labour, and flogging (except as a punishment for breaches of prison discipline), and then went on to present a comprehensive system for the punishment and treatment of offenders. Prisons still lay at the centre of the system, and the rules for their management were set out. But penal institutions now included remand centres, remand homes, detention centres, and borstal institutions. The system of punishment also encompassed fines, recognizances, probation, special powers relating to young persons, special powers relating to persistent offenders, detailed procedures for the granting of remission for good conduct and release on licence, and the treatment of persons of unsound mind and mental defectives. This piece of legislation, including the details of the earlier Acts it amended or repealed, took over a hundred pages of the standard HMSO *Public General Acts* of 1948. Yet many of those who had involved themselves in the movement for penal reform felt that the system it enshrined included one last anomalous relic of the penal past which had to be abolished: the death penalty.

The Abolition of Capital Punishment

In focusing our attention on the death penalty, we are entering an area which is still, and will probably continue to be, one of lively public debate. As we have seen, until the early nineteenth century England and Wales retained the death penalty for a large number of offences, while in the sixteenth and seventeenth centuries the actual levels of execution, most of those being hanged having been found guilty of property offences, were very high. Since the middle of the nineteenth century, however, debate has centred on the abolition of capital punishment for murder, and it is this which gives discussion of the issue its unique emotive tone. Most people, abolitionist or otherwise, would accept that wilful murder is the most dreadful of offences, and it is the need to meet this most dreadful of crimes with the most dreadful of punishments which lies at the heart of the retentionist case. Conversely, capital punishment can be seen as a punishment apart, in the same way as murder can be seen as a crime apart. Thus an Amnesty International Report on the death penalty could claim agreement that

> the death penalty is unique as a punishment, quite separate from all other punishments and not simply distinguishable from them in degree of severity. This point has a direct bearing on all consideration of alternatives to the death penalty.[21]

It is the unique status of the infliction of death as a penalty which gives it, to modern European eyes, a certain fascination. Beneath the various attitudes to it there lurk some fundamental strands of our wider attitudes to the social order. This provides yet further justification for our giving detailed attention to the arguments surrounding the death penalty in twentieth-century Britain.

The arguments for and against the use of the death penalty were established in the nineteenth century, and in effect the positions set out then are still with us.[22] The major abolitionist arguments are threefold. The first is a moral one: the taking of life as punishment for a crime is ethically wrong, whether the ethics in question are Christian or those more generally of the civilized west. The second argument is a more practical one: capital punishment is irreversible.

If a mistake is made in the judicial process which results in an execution, there is no way of rectifying it. Thirdly, there is no other punishment which inflicts so much suffering on innocent people, notably the family of the person being executed. A number of lesser arguments have been employed by abolitionists, among them, interestingly, the suggestion that no punishment has had such an effect on the men charged with carrying it out. Obviously, the memoirs of some nineteenth-century hangmen demonstrate a rather robust attitude to the whole business: conversely, some of those who have put their thoughts down more recently, notably prison governors, have been less enthusiastic. Another sentiment sometimes expressed by abolitionists is that the execution itself or the knowledge that a murder trial might lead to an execution, given the taste of the media for sensation, might create an unhealthy atmosphere which at the very best would lead to morbidity and which at the worst would lead to a pandering to the human race's more sadistic impulses.

The main components of the retentionist case are equally familiar. Again, there is a moral position. Some crimes (since the mid nineteenth century, in effect murder) are so heinous as to demand stringent retribution: in fact, the retributionist argument is probably to be found at its most vocal when the case for the capital punishment of murderers is being discussed. Also we return to the idea so often connected with retributionist arguments, that certain types of punishment help reinforce social mores. Related to this is the knowledge that, on the evidence of most polls conducted during this century, the majority of the British public is in favour of capital punishment for murder. Another argument, frequently deployed in newspapers and in political debate, is that the abolition of capital punishment may be a good idea in the abstract, but that current crime levels mean that the present time is not a propitious one to introduce it. Lastly, and perhaps more importantly, comes the deterrent argument. Not only is there no satisfactory alternative to the death penalty on moral grounds, but it is also seen as being uniquely effective in deterring certain types of potential murderer. It is, perhaps, this last argument which has given rise to the most detailed debate. The most telling abolitionist point here is that most murders are crimes of impulse (if not passion) carried out by people who are not professional criminals, a type of offence whose perpetrators are among the least likely to have their actions inhibited by fear of a deterrent punishment. The retributionist response would be to take this point, but to suggest that without capital punishment professional criminals would feel far fewer constraints on taking life while committing other crimes, notably robbery.

The abolition of capital punishment in Britain came, as we shall see, in 1965. But it is important to grasp (not least because it was a point frequently made by abolitionists) that a number of other countries, mainly in Europe and South America, had abolished the death penalty at an earlier date. E. Roy Calvert, reviewing the situation in 1927, listed the countries where, although it might be retained for treason or as a punishment under emergency powers or martial law, capital punishment was not included in the normal penal code. Calvert's analysis argued that Austria had abolished the death penalty for all normal purposes in 1918. In Belgium, although capital punishment for murder was on the statute book, there had been no executions since 1862. Similarly Denmark, despite the continued presence of the death penalty in the penal code, had experienced no executions since 1892, and Finland (apart from during a brief period of martial law in 1918) since 1826. Capital punishment had been abolished in the Netherlands in 1870, in Italy in 1889 (it was revived under fascism). Lithuania had abolished it in 1922; Norway in 1905; Portugal in 1867; Romania in 1865; Sweden in 1921; Argentina in 1922; Brazil in 1891; Ecuador in 1895. It was obvious that by the time Calvert wrote a wide variety of states were able to do without the death penalty for normal purposes. This was important for two reasons. Firstly, abolitionists could argue these foreign examples as moral exemplars. Secondly, statistics were now available to attack the retentionists' insistence on the unique value of the death penalty as a deterrent. Runs of figures for countries as diverse as Norway and Italy provided demonstrations of how the abolition of the death penalty for murder was followed by a drop in the number of homicides. In Italy, for example, homicides in 1880–4, a few years before abolition, were running at 10.64 per 100,000 of population, but had dropped to 2.75 per 100,000 (still a very high figure by Northern European standards) by 1919. Even more illumination could be gathered from the United States, where some states had abolished the death penalty, and others had not. The five highest rates, between 10.90 and 12.90 per 100,000, were experienced by Virginia, Kentucky, California, Southern California and Montana, all of which retained the death penalty. Such figures provided grounds for arguing that whatever else the death penalty may have been doing, it did not seem to be deterring murderers.[23]

The debate on capital punishment in England really began early in the nineteenth century when attempts were made to dismantle the Bloody Code. That task accomplished, from around 1850 the debate centred mainly on the abolition of capital punishment for murder. The subject was, indeed, a matter of continuous debate from the 1840s, at the end of which decade William Ewart, leader of the campaign for complete abolition, attempted to introduce a bill to that effect into the Commons. He was unsuccessful, but debate continued both inside and outside parliament and in 1864 a Royal Commission was appointed to consider the issue. Once again Ewart, aided as previously by John Bright, was the leading proponent of the abolitionist position. The Commission accepted that capital punishment for treason should be retained, and that the real area of contention was whether it should be abolished for murder. The solution envisaged was that murder, following the example of the United States, should be divided into degrees, with capital punishment retained for first degree murder. Nothing came of this idea, nor of other measures that were discussed, although the Commission's deliberations did have one important outcome: public execution was abolished in 1868. A Select Committee of 1874, which also turned to looking at the adoption of a subdivision of murder into degrees, had a similar lack of success.

The issue remained a live one, however, surfacing again in a parliamentary debate of 1877, when the abolitionist case was raised once more. Ewart was dead by then, but a number of MPs spoke in favour of abolition, one of them, J. W. Pease, arguing that 'at no distant date capital punishment will no longer exist'.[24] Such a notion was obviously a little optimistic, yet such sentiments do remind us of the forward-looking nature of much Victorian social thinking. Needless to say, this view was not shared by the government spokesman, Attorney-General Sir John Holker, who spoke from a strongly deterrent position. Pease again sought abolition in 1881, encouraged by the arrival of a Liberal government. He was again defeated.

This account of the fortunes of the nineteenth-century parliamentary debates on abolition serves to remind us that the removal of the death penalty for murder, still a matter of contention and parliamentary votes as I write, is something which has been considered for some time. We must reiterate that most of the current arguments for and against were already familiar over a century ago: indeed, one commentator noted of the 1877 campaign that, 'the debate was a vigorous one. In it, nearly every argument, pro and con, that has been made before or since, was used.'[25] But after about 1881 the issue seems to have run out of steam, at least at a parliamentary level, although the formation of the Penal Reform League in 1907 did demonstrate a continued public interest in penological matters.

Abolition was raised again as a parliamentary issue in the 1920s, however, and its lack of progress in parliament led to the formation in 1927 of the National Council for the Abolition of the Death Penalty. The Council's first secretary and moving genius was a twenty-seven year old civil servant named Roy Calvert, who immediately led the Council into an active propaganda campaign outside parliament, perhaps the best known document of this period being his *Capital Punishment in the Twentieth Century*, 1927. The pressure for reform led in October 1929 to a full-scale debate on capital punishment, and the appointment of a parliamentary Select Committee to consider the matter. The Committee, which began its real work in January 1930, interviewed numerous witnesses, and eventually produced 500 pages of printed evidence, complemented by 100 pages of appendices. The eventual report stated that 'capital punishment may be abolished in this country without endangering life or property, or impairing the security of society'.[26] But no action was taken on the strength of the report, and the Committee's credibility had already been wrecked by the walk-out of six of its Conservative members. The Labour government, which was to fall in August 1931, allowed no debate on the report which, however, stood as a powerful document in support of the abolitionist cause.

Pressure was maintained throughout the 1930s, with propaganda constantly being aimed at the public. The eccentric Mrs Violet van der Elst would harangue the crowds gathered outside prisons where executions were being held, and distribute abolitionist handbills among them. The Archbishop of York, William Temple, wrote a widely read abolitionist tract. Between 1934 and 1939 a journal, *The Penal Reformer*, regularly carried abolitionist articles. The parliamentary campaign was revived in 1938, when Vyvyan Adams launched a debate on the subject. The familiar arguments were deployed by both sides, and at one point it seemed possible that parliament might legislate to abolish the death penalty for a trial period of five years. The obvious course was to attempt to add abolition to the Criminal Justice Bill, which by the spring of 1939 was being considered by a standing committee. This course was, however, blocked and the outbreak of war in the September of that year effectively put an end to debate of the issue. The coming of peace and the entry into office of a strong Labour government in 1945 was to see its revival.

The immediate cause of this revival was the Criminal Justice Bill, itself re-emerging into the post-war sunlight. At this point the most active champion of the abolitionist cause was Sydney Silverman, Labour member for Nelson and Colne. His motion for introducing a clause into the Bill suspending capital punishment was seconded by the Conservative MP Christopher Hollis, a neat demonstration of the laudable, if sometimes hollow convention that capital punishment is a non-party issue. In the event the clause, recommending the suspension of the death penalty for a trial period of five years, passed the Commons but was rejected by the Lords. A counter-proposal, which returned to the notion of introducing degrees of murder, failed, and the Criminal Justice Act 1948 was passed without any alteration of the law relating to capital punishment. In 1949, however, yet another Royal Commission on Capital Punishment was appointed, and eventually submitted its report in 1953. The Commission decided to limit itself mainly to the problem of considering degrees of murder, although in the last resort it was forced to accept that abolition was the underlying issue. The whole issue seems to have hung fire on a parliamentary level, but public opinion was suddenly stirred by two controversial murder cases. The first involved Timothy Evans and John Christie. Evans was executed in 1950 for the murder of his child (his wife had also died) but during the trial withdrew an earlier confession, and accused one of his neighbours, Christie, of being the murderer. In 1953 Christie was tried for the murder of six women, including his wife, and at the trial confessed to killing Evans's wife, although he denied killing the child. Despite this denial, the case obviously threw considerable doubt on Evans's guilt. The second controversial case was that of Derek Bentley. Bentley was hanged, also in 1953, as an accomplice in the murder of a police officer (the actual murderer was aged under eighteen, and hence could not be capitally punished) even though he was probably in custody when the fatal shooting took place. The execution in 1955 of Ruth Ellis, the last woman to be hanged in England, also caught the public's attention.

These cases perhaps illustrate how, in recent centuries, individual incidents can have a major impact on debate over punishment. Most often, as in the aftermath of the 1862 garrotting panic, these incidents are such as to encourage a more punitive attitude. If a number of particularly heinous and well publicized child murders had occurred in the early 1950s the abolitionist cause would have suffered a major setback. As it was, they found the time ripe to renew their campaign. The Howard League for Penal Reform (formed in 1948 when the Howard Association and the National Council for the Abolition of Capital Punishment merged) ground into action, Arthur Koestler's *Reflections on Hanging* added an important, if emotive, new work to the abolitionist canon, and the parliamentary campaign (already reinstigated by Silverman early in 1955) was intensified. On 15 November 1955 Silverman introduced a Bill proposing the abolition of capital punishment, this being debated on 16 February 1956. The arguments, once again, were the familiar ones. Silverman accepted this:

> I have taken part in too many of these debates to feel it possible to advance anything very new . . . the truth of the matter is that there are very few arguments either way on this issue, that most of us know them, and that we have made our own individual assessments, where in the end the balance of arguments lies.[27]

The Bill passed the Commons, but was heavily defeated in the Lords. The end product was a compromise, the Homicide Act 1957. This specified six varieties of capital murder: murder in the course of theft; murder by shooting or causing an explosion; murder in the course of resisting an arrest or making an escape; murder of a police officer in the course of his duties, or of a person assisting him; the same in relation to prison officers; and repeated murders. This removed about three quarters of the types of murder previously subject to it from capital punishment. The first execution under the new legislation took place on 23 July 1957.

The 1957 Act, as might have been expected, was found to be unsatisfactory, as making some of the distinctions between the various types of murder was very difficult. Moreover, the actual levels of execution under the Act were so low as to amount to a near abolition in any case: two hangings in 1957, five in 1958, five in 1959. In total, thirty-eight persons were hanged in England and Wales between 1955 and 1964. Whatever its symbolic importance, in practical terms capital punishment was obviously a little-used sanction. After the 1964 election, Silverman and his allies renewed their attempts at abolition. His Murder (Abolition of the Death Penalty) Bill had a stormy passage through the Commons. It was introduced as a private member's Bill, and came up for its second reading on 21 December 1964. From the outset it was obvious that no new arguments were going to be deployed. Indeed, Silverman's ability to speak at length without recourse to notes might well be taken as a symbol of the degree to which most of the participants in the debate were familiar with the issues. Henry Brooke, a former Home Secretary not noted for his radical proclivities, made a speech stating that he was now convinced that capital punishment was no longer justifiable. The rational retentionist case was made by Sir Peter Rawlinson, the former Conservative Solicitor-General, the less rational one by such Conservatives as Brigadier Terence Clarke, Member for Portsmouth West. The Bill went through its second reading by 358 votes in favour to 170 against.

The Bill encountered a number of delays, which gave its opponents a chance to rally their forces, but was eventually passed to the House of Lords, which was in a generally reforming mood (their Lordships had just taken a liberal view on legislation affecting homosexuality). The Bill passed its second reading in the Upper House by a majority of two to one, receiving the Royal Assent on 8 November 1965. Initially abolition was to be for a trial period of five years, but despite worry over the rising crime levels of the late

1960s, and some well-publicized murders (notably the shooting of three London policemen in 1966) the period was subsequently extended indefinitely. After over a century of debate, Britain had joined those nations which had chosen, for all practical purposes, to dispense with the death penalty.

Our treatment of the abolition of capital punishment has been a long one, longer perhaps than the frequency with which the death penalty has been applied over the last century might justify. Yet such a lengthy treatment is clearly deserved. Capital punishment is in a certain sense symbolic, and abolitionists and retentionists are likely to have opposite views on a number of other penal (and, indeed, wider) issues. Secondly, the debate has been useful in demonstrating the longevity of some of the attitudes deployed about punishment: the arguments for and against abolition were established over a century ago, and it is unlikely that new ones will be added to them. Yet each generation, it seems, discovers them anew. Thirdly, the campaign for abolition and the opposition it aroused provide the most dramatic evidence of that process which, it would seem, first became important in the later eighteenth century, and which helps set the earlier penal world apart from ours: the way in which the punishment of criminals has become a matter of public debate, of pressure groups, of opinion polls. Capital punishment is an issue, more than any other in penal debate, which arouses the emotions, and as has been pointed out 'emotional issues are likely to be "popular" issues in the sense that the layman feels at home with them and competent to pronounce upon them', and that they evoke 'widespread public interest of a sort not present when technical or more mundane questions are raised'.[28] It is this tendency to view the issue in emotive terms which makes it especially easy for so many people who have commented on the abolition of the death penalty for murder to reject rational arguments against their position. Unfortunately, such a rejection is not present merely when it is the death penalty which is under discussion: it also affects reactions to the more 'technical or mundane' aspects of judicial punishment and crime control. It is to these matters that we shall turn next.

Towards the Crisis

We return to the propositions with which we began our introduction. Our system of punishment is facing a crisis, and this crisis is at its most marked in our prisons.[29] Over the past forty years the problems surrounding our gaols have got steadily worse. Their population has risen. In 1945, the average daily prison population in England and Wales was 12,910. In 1950 it had risen to 20,474; in 1960 to 27,099; in 1965 to 29,580; in 1975 to 39,820; in 1985 to 46,234; and in 1986 to 46,900. The extent of this increase becomes obvious when it is contrasted with the overall increase in the population of England and Wales, this rising from 42,636,000 in 1945 to 50,075,000 in 1986. Thus in a period when the national population rose by 17 per cent, that of the nation's prisons rose by 263 per cent. The costs of imprisonment rose more drastically than the number of prison inmates. In 1945 the gross expenditure on the prison service in England and Wales was £2,985,000. By 1955–6 this had risen to £10,345,000 gross; by 1965–6 to £33,781,000 gross; by 1975–6 to £202,847,000 net; and by 1986 to £786,500,000. In the financial year 1984–5 the Scottish prison system cost a further £5,391,000. In that year, it cost an average £256 a week to keep a prisoner in a gaol in England and Wales, although this average masked wide variations in the cost of incarceration in different types of institution: £482 in a dispersal prison, in which maximum security prisoners would be placed; £363 in a women's prison; £164 in an adult open prison. A large proportion of these ever increasing costs are accounted for by staff salaries, for the number of prison officers has been rising at a faster rate than the number of prisoners. In 1985, it was noted that whereas the number of prisoners had trebled since the Second World War, the number of uniformed staff had increased eightfold.[30]

Despite the money spent on the system, our prisons are badly overcrowded. In 1986, it will be remembered, there were 46,900 prisoners occupying accommodation for 40,811. This overcrowding was not, of course, spread evenly throughout the prison system. Thus, in March 1986, dispersal prisons, open prisons for men, youth custody centres for men and women alike and detention centres all had spare capacity. But remand centres and prisons for men were 48 per cent over-occupied, local prisons for men 47 per cent over-occupied, and prisons for women 27 per cent over-occupied.

The practice of putting prisoners two or three to a cell was noted and regretted as a problem in immediate post-war prison commissioners' reports, and by the late 1960s had assumed the status of a permanent blight on the prison system. In some of our prisons, three men are kept in a cell for twenty-three hours at a stretch, the cell in question having frequently been designed for a single occupant in the nineteenth century. They have to urinate and defecate in each others' company into a plastic bucket in the cell, which will be slopped out at intervals. They are allowed one bath a week. The staffing levels in the more overcrowded prisons are frequently too low to allow prisoners access to recreational facilities, training, or work. The staff in any case are becoming increasingly alienated from and cynical about their duties which, even for the more idealistic of them, cannot but assume something of the nature of keeping the lid on a human dustbin.

This situation is made even more remarkable in that it arises in part because the British are apparently keener than most of their European neighbours to put their fellow citizens into prison. A Labour Party report of 1982 showed that in the United Kingdom as a whole 80 per 100,000 of the population were convicted prisoners. This compared with 67.1 per 100,000 in West Germany; 44.8 in Denmark; 39.4 in France; 32 in Eire; 31.67 in Belgium; 21.8 in Italy; and 13.4 in the Netherlands. Other studies have noted that societies as diverse as Sweden, Ontario and Japan manage to survive with far fewer of their members incarcerated than in Britain. It may be, of course, that the British are a uniquely wicked race in need of a high level of incarceration: conversely, it may simply be that putting offenders in prison is the normal thing to do in Britain. Certainly countries experiencing similar increases in crime to Britain's have not invariably experienced a similar rise in prison population. Thus in Australia the crime rate rose by 180 per cent between 1960 and 1979, while England and Wales's rose by an almost identical 177 per cent. In Australia the number of prisoners increased by 9 per cent, in England 45 per cent.[31] Too much should not perhaps be made of relatively unsophisticated international comparisons; even so, the high levels of imprisonment in Britain are striking.

The current problems in Britain's gaols have come about despite thirty years of concern over the prison system, and of devising means to improve it. As early as 1959 the realization that the prison system was showing signs of strain under mounting pressures led to the publication of a government White Paper, *Penal Practice in a Changing Society*, generally accepted as being largely the work of Sir Lionel Fox, Chairman of the Prison Commissioners from 1942. The paper identified the crux of the problems facing the prison system as the treatment of persistent offenders, and especially the permanent recidivist, and geared its recommendations to this issue. With its emphasis on the need for more research into crime and punishment, and its call for a more fundamental review of penal philosophy and practices, the White Paper was a forward-looking document, in many ways reminiscent of the Paterson era in which Fox had been nurtured. As ever, though, little of the more radical measures were implemented and the call for a thoroughgoing review of the penal system was dropped. The main outcome of the Paper, indeed, was the building of a number of new closed prisons.

Despite its impact (some of the more effusive commentators thought it comparable to the Gladstone Committee report in its significance), *Penal Practice in a Changing Society* has been criticized for failing to address some of the central problems. As the authors of a study of Albany Prison, one of the fruits of the report, have put it:

> it expected that its aims could be achieved by new buildings and staff training, and without a major overhaul of the creaking administrative structure and unwieldy procedures which had grown up over three quarters of a century. Its concern for science and professionalisation was directed solely to the understanding of the causes of crime and finding a better way of treating it, not at all with the management of the prison system itself and the control of the establishments which make it up.[32]

Fox's views on penal policy had been formed during the Paterson era, and his main concern, as we have noted, was the treatment and reformation of recidivists. The realities of the years following 1959, however, dictated that the slender resources of the system had to be devoted to containment (in particular perimeter security) and modern methods of prison management. The abolition of the Prison Commission and the merger of its structure into the Home Office as the Prison Department in 1963 paved the way for the final downgrading of the ideals of Paterson's generation.

One sign of the strains in the prison system was the growing number of escapes. In 1946 there were 864 escapes and attempted escapes. In 1964 there were 2,090. The worries provoked by these statistics were sharply focused by a series of spectacular escapes in the mid 1960s. In August 1964 a group of men broke into Birmingham prison and released the train robber Charles Wilson, who was serving a thirty year sentence. In July 1965 another Great Train Robber, Ronald Biggs, was sprung from Wandsworth. In late 1965 and early 1966 soldiers patrolled Durham gaol and armed police were brought into Leicester in response to fears of similar coups. In October 1966 George Blake, a spy, escaped from Dartmoor, and later that year Frank Mitchell, serving a life sentence for robbery with violence, escaped from Dartmoor. The escape of Blake, however, had already prompted action. It now seemed that the prison system was unable even to perform the basic function of containment, and the Home Secretary, Roy Jenkins, appointed a Committee of Enquiry under Earl Mountbatten of Burma to inquire into the escapes and make recommendations on how prison security might be improved. Mountbatten was appointed on 24 October 1966, and had his report published in fifty-nine days, after visiting seventeen establishments and taking evidence from a wide variety of individuals and organizations.

The recommendations of the report were various. The most important of them were the recommendations that prisoners should be put into four categories, A to D in descending order of risk to security, and that each should be sent to prison with an appropriate regime. The second was that all category A prisoners should be placed in a new maximum security prison to be built on the Isle of Wight, with the option of opening a second maximum security prison should the number of category A prisoners warrant it. The maximum security prison should have a strong perimeter, the staff should have special training, and modern security aids should be used alongside such traditional ones as guard dogs. The report also stressed the need for better lines of communication between the head office of the Prison Department and prison governors, and between the governors and their staff. Despite its emphasis on security (understandably, given the Committee's remit) the Mountbatten Report recognized the importance of rehabilitative work and expressed the opinion that many people currently imprisoned under closed conditions might safely be transferred to open ones, recognized the viability of outside working parties and even suggested the possibility of domestic visits for prisoners. The report was also responsible for expediting some much needed improvements in the career structure of the uniformed staff.

As is in the nature of such things, the report's recommendations were only partially implemented. In particular, the plan for a single high-security prison was dropped as too inflexible, and replaced with the dispersal of category A prisoners in maximum security areas in various prisons. The policy of dispersal was a controversial one, opposed from the start by the POA, and receiving a mixed reaction from penologists and criminologists. Certainly, whatever the intrinsic benefits of the idea, its actual implementation was disruptive and caused problems for staff and prisoners alike. The wider issue of the imprisonment of offenders serving long sentences in maximum security conditions obviously needed further thinking, and on 13 March 1967 a sub-committee appointed for this task met for the first time under the chairmanship of Sir Leon Radzinowicz. The Radzinowicz Committee's report, published in 1968, was much wider ranging than the Mountbatten Report, and came down firmly in favour of dispersal. Despite this, its overall impact was to continue the tendency towards a greater stress on security and a greater emphasis on managerial efficiency in prisons. A management review team was set up in 1968, and in 1969 published a new White Paper, *People in Prison*. This recommended a new command structure at the centre of the system, with a subordinate layer of administration based on four regional offices. The optimism of the first half of the twentieth century had been replaced by a new ethos founded on preventive rigour and tight management.

The whole of the prison system became more security conscious, and the growing emphasis on containment soon led to an erosion of any ideals of reformation or rehabilitation. The escapes of the mid 1960s, aided as some of them were by teams of criminals outside the prisons, caused considerable paranoia among the agents of law enforcement. Consider the following remarkable statement from the Chief Constable of Durham, that friends of the inmates of Durham Prison

> were prepared to launch something in the nature of a full-scale military attack, even to the extent of using tanks, bombs, and what the army describes as limited atomic weapons. Once armoured vehicles had breached the gates, there would be nothing to stop them. A couple of tanks could easily come through the streets of Durham unchallenged. Nothing is too extravagent.[33]

The impact of this extreme insistence on security can be neatly illustrated by reference to developments in one prison, Albany on the Isle of Wight, originally planned in 1961 as a medium security prison to replace Dartmoor with accommodation for 480 long-term repeated offenders. The first prisoners were admitted in 1967. That year an electronic unlocking system that allowed prisoners to go to the lavatory at night was installed, while the twelve-foot high security fence was replaced by a seventeen-foot one. On Albany's conversion to a dispersal prison in 1968, dog handlers and dogs arrived. A new security fence twenty feet high was constructed, as was a strengthened gatehouse, while TV surveillance cameras, high mast lighting, geophonic alarms and a control room were installed. In 1973 the perimeter fence was modified into a wall. None of this prevented continual disturbances by the prisoners between 1971 and 1985, in the October of which year the POA reported that over forty staff had been assaulted since January. Dartmoor, one notes, has not yet been replaced.[34]

One group which, naturally enough, became increasingly alarmed over conditions within prisons were the prison officers. As we have suggested, there were already incipient rifts between the prison officers and the higher echelons of the prison system before the outbreak of the Second World War, and the situation since 1945 had done little to ease them. As Vivien Stern noted:

> The prerequisite for a constructive and humane prison system would seem to be well-trained and committed staff who get satisfaction from their work

and feel that the difficult and dangerous job they do is understood and appreciated by those in authority over them.[35]

Sadly, this prerequisite is clearly lacking. A report published in March 1986 confirmed the continuation of certain salient features among the discipline (i.e. uniformed non-specialist) officers. These tended to have only a low educational profile, in terms of formal qualifications: 40 per cent had none, and 30 per cent merely three O-levels. Formal qualifications are not of course the only desirable attributes in a prison officer, but these low educational levels do seem to be reflected in the low esteem in which officers hold training, whether for themselves or for prisoners. A majority had a background in the armed services, many of them as regulars. Such people, whatever virtues they may possess, are unlikely to have a flexible or reflective attitude to punishment or crime control, while in fairness it should be remembered that current conditions in Britain's gaols are unlikely to encourage the flourishing of such attitudes. The drift of research is that prison officers find that the reality of working in prisons confirms them in their scepticism about the prison system in general and the hope of reforming prisoners in particular, especially as such hope is usually expressed in directives from above. Given the problems inherent in the job, it is understandable that the prison officers' frustrations are most often expressed along two familiar lines of argument: everything is done for prisoners, and nothing for prison officers; and that the role of the Home Office is to devise schemes to prevent the officers from doing their job properly.

Under such conditions, it is little wonder that prisons can only run on the basis of two uneasy truces: one between the prison officers and the inmates, and one between the prison officers and the governor. The impression is that, in many respects, many prison officers are doing their time as much as the inmates are. Their basic object is to get through the day with the minimum of trouble, and this implies an adherence to routine and an acceptance of those bendings of the rules without which most complex institutions are incapable of functioning. The intrusion into such a situation of specialists like psychologists or psychiatrists, or of new instructions from the Home Office or from the governor, are bound to cause resentment. But, whatever sympathy one might have for the prison officers' position, it remains clear that the POA has become one of the most powerful and most difficult groups of organized labour in Britain, and that, interestingly in a period when trade union rights have been attacked with fairly consistent success, this situation has prompted little governmental attention or adverse comment in the media. The 1970s were a very bad period for industrial relations in prisons, with a peak of 119 instances of industrial action by POA branches in 1978. Problems continued into the next decade, a work to rule over manning levels in 1986, which had considerably wider ramifications for the system, proving especially difficult. One of the most persistent problems was officers' concern about their overtime pay which, together with shift allowance and weekend premiums, might under ideal circumstances allow them to almost double their salaries. Protection of overtime and other bonuses led to the retention of many restrictive practices by officers, and it remains to be seen how far the 'Fresh Start' initiative, one of whose objectives was the rationalization of officers' pay, will have any lasting impact on industrial relations in Britain's prisons.

Given the worsening situation in the prisons it is hardly surprising that there have been a number of initiatives aimed at bringing down the proportion of convicted offenders sentenced to imprisonment. Current practice in England and Wales seems to be set against the alternative method of easing the crisis in the prisons, namely awarding shorter sentences. Investigation of alternatives, however, has seen a number of fruitful innovations, and has also led, on a more theoretical level, to wider debate on the opportunities for decarceration. This debate, however, has so far been of little practical importance: the general tone of penal policy since the late 1970s has been pessimistic, and the welfare and treatment aspects of the way we treat offenders have been downgraded.[36]

Nevertheless, a number of alternatives to imprisonment continue to flourish. The probation service continues to deal with numerous offenders, although the proportion of the total of offenders sentenced for an indictable offence and subsequently put on probation declined by 50 per cent between 1960 and 1981, by which date only 7 per cent of such offenders were made subject to a probation order. The main elements in a probation order remained what they had always been: an order can only be made with the consent of the offender, it is intended to be for the offender's benefit, and the court making the order can impose conditions on the offender. These conditions can vary: offenders might be directed to receive some sort of treatment; they might be required to take part in some potentially helpful activity, such as attending a day centre or participating in an employment project; or they might have some restriction placed upon them, such as being banned from a football ground. It is these elements of control which are seen as being especially useful elements in the probation order. Evaluating the usefulness of probation as opposed to other forms of punishment is difficult, but a study of the sentencing of adult males published in 1981 reached some interesting conclusions. Probation was not especially effective in reducing reconviction rates for first offenders, but it was relatively effective for those with between two and four previous convictions, and was as ineffective as imprisonment in deterring those with over five convictions from committing further offences. Probation, it would therefore seem, is still a viable way of treating offenders.[37]

While probation was a long established method of dealing with criminals, the last twenty years have also seen two major innovations in the range of punishments. The first of these is the suspended sentence. This was introduced in 1967, the objective being to achieve the deterrent effects of a short or medium sentence without actually putting the offender into prison. Thus a court can, when sentencing up to two years' imprisonment, suspend the beginning of the sentence for a period of up to two years. Offenders so sentenced who are not convicted within the set period are allowed to remain free. Despite the original intention of keeping people who would otherwise have received a custodial sentence out of prison, the courts rapidly began to use suspended sentences against convicted offenders who would not invariably have received a custodial sentence. By 1968, over half of those under suspended sentences would otherwise have been fined, and about one in seven put on probation. In fact, it could be argued that the use of suspended sentences has actually increased the prison population: about a third of suspended sentences are activated on the reconviction of the offender, which means that a substantial number of people who would otherwise have been fined are imprisoned.[38] Study of reconviction rates also suggests that suspended sentences are not an entire success. For first offenders, reconviction for those under suspended sentences were more numerous than might have been anticipated for the type of offence for which they were convicted, while the results for offenders with one to four previous convictions were also poor.[39]

Another innovation aimed at keeping convicted offenders outside prison was the Community Service Order. This is a device whereby a convicted offender, with his or her consent, spends a set number of hours (normally between 100 and 150) doing unpaid work of benefit to the community within a period of a year. Modelled to some extent on probation orders, the Community Service Order can only be made in respect to an offence punishable by a custodial sentence, and a breach of such an order might lead to imprisonment. This sentencing option rapidly became popular, and was seen as being especially appropriate for offenders aged less than twenty-one. It has a number of virtues. Firstly, it is obviously much cheaper than putting an offender into custody, while it is marginally cheaper to supervise than a probation order. It does succeed in keeping offenders out of prison, an especially important consideration given the frequency with which it is applied to young offenders. It can be portrayed as being useful. And it involves a visible element of reparation: the 'debt to society' can be seen to be repaid. There are, of course, problems with the Community Service Order: some would argue that it is a soft line to take against offenders; there are some types of offenders, notably drug or alcohol addicts, with whom it seems to be less successful; and it is not having a totally effective role in diminishing the prison population. Yet there is little doubt that it will continue to be widely used, even if, as investigations carried out in 1976 suggest, there is little evidence that Community Service Orders reduce rates of reconviction among those experiencing them.[40]

As the above paragraph suggests, one area of constant concern, and constant innovation, lay in the punishment and treatment of young offenders. The Victorian invention of juvenile delinquency, and of the presence of special measures aimed at the young offender, was carried on by the 1908 Act and became a constant of later penal policy. Post-1945 developments continued to demonstrate a search for new initiatives. One of these was the detention centre. The Criminal Justice Act 1948 ended corporal punishment as a sentence for juveniles, and also attempted to restrict the power of the courts to send young people to prison. The gap thus created was to be filled by detention centres. These were intended, as the then Home Secretary, Chuter Ede, explained in 1947, to give a 'short but sharp reminder that he is getting into ways that will lead him to disaster' to an offender for whom it was felt that a fine or probation would be too lenient, and imprisonment too serious a punishment.[41] The detention centre is still with us, as is the concept of 'short but sharp' punishment. Indeed, one of the major outcomes of the Criminal Justice Act 1982 – which saw the end of borstal training – was to confirm the detention centre's role as the first-stage penal establishment for young people.[42]

The treatment approach to young offenders was also well established, and was enshrined in a number of publications. In 1965 a White Paper, *The Child, the Family and the Young Offender*, suggested radical changes in the treatment of young offenders, but encountered strong, and not unreasonable, resistance from a number of quarters. A second White Paper, *Children in Trouble*, was presented to Parliament in 1968. This was considered less extreme, and a number of its recommendations were incorporated into the Children and Young Persons Act 1969. This was a long and complex piece of legislation, but its overall intent was to rehabilitate through treatment. To this end, it offered a wide range of options to the courts when they dealt with young offenders: binding over, supervision orders, care orders, sending to a community home. None of these prevented a massive rise in the number of young offenders sent into custody (there was a 100 per cent rise between 1972 and 1982 in 14- to 16-year-olds), while dissatisfaction grew with the sentencing structure of the 1969 Act, especially in juvenile courts dealing with offenders aged under 17. It was felt that the Act lacked clarity, and the concept of intermediate treatment which it introduced was conceptually vague and uncertain in content. The provisions of the Criminal Justice Act 1982 dealing with young offenders were, it was hoped, going to offer clarity. Youth custody replaced borstal training and subsequently imprisonment of those aged between 17 and 21, but the commitment was still to try to find alternatives to custody for young offenders. In fact, the workings of the 1982 Act proved that it too had ambiguities, while, as one author of a research report on the working of the Act has commented, 'whether the silent majority of those affected, the young defendants . . . were aware of any difference at all is a matter which history is likely to leave unrecorded'.[43] Dealing with the young offender apparently involves as many problems as does dealing with his or her adult counterpart.

Thus the current situation as far as the judicial punishment of criminals is concerned is profoundly unsatisfactory, and is likely to remain so. Certainly, if the possible connection between social structure and crime to which we alluded in the introduction to this work has any force, there is little ground for optimism. It is possible that a socialist millennium will arrive and cause a diminution of crime by ending economic inequality and alienation. It is also possible that a full flourishing of the capitalist enterprise culture will make everyone so wealthy that the same outcome will ensue. Given that neither of these eventualities seems very likely, however, our assumption must be that English society will continue much as it now is, will experience a broadly similar type of criminality, and will continue with much the same policies in punishing and treating criminals.

This situation will be compounded by two factors. The first of these is that the general public will understandably think about crime and punishment in terms of gut reactions rather than in a more reflective fashion. The second, however, is that those agencies and people upon which innovations in and clear thinking about punishment depend (let alone such opinion moulders as the popular press) are, once again understandably, attached to set routines or have entrenched attitudes and interests. Most seriously, our political leaders, realizing that creative thinking over law and order issues is likely to lose them votes, are unlikely to mastermind any major breakthroughs in judicial punishment. History shows that such changes can occur; but there is little in our current situation to indicate that many will be forthcoming in the near future.

Yet despite our pessimism on this point it is obvious that a number of strategies are currently being mooted which might ameliorate the penal crisis. The first of these is the widely acknowledged need to put fewer people into prison. As we have noted, offenders are more likely to be imprisoned after conviction in the United Kingdom than in most comparable Western European states. We must reiterate that there are problems with comparisons of this type: yet if Belgium, West Germany, Holland and France can imprison a lower proportion of their population than does Britain, and yet not be noticeably less secure societies, there seems little reason why Britain should not follow their lead. Over the past two decades a considerable literature has grown up (much of it originating from the United States) arguing the need for decarceration and of a more urgent search for alternatives to prison (e.g. Dodge, 1979; Stanley and Baginsky 1984; Scull 1984; Pointing, 1986). The logic of our current situation would seem to push us in the same direction. This, of course, introduces another problem: sentencing policy. This subject, as crucial to our understanding of the current situation as it is to our understanding of the eighteenth century's, has also attracted some serious attention in recent years.[44] What emerges from these studies is that, whatever disparities there may be between the proportions of sentences awarded by different courts, the rationale upon which any individual sentence is based is usually very similar to that which obtained in the early modern period. The sentence awarded will be affected by the age, perhaps sex, and previous record of the offender; on the perceived gravity of the crime; on a desire to make examples if the crime is thought serious, or if there is a short-term scare about crime in general; and, conversely, on any ameliorating circumstances. Punishments may have changed, but the basis upon which they are awarded shows considerable continuity.

Sentencing also takes place in a context of public concern, and, if in a very generalized way, public interest in crime and punishment remains high. A recent survey has shown that out of a sample of nearly 1,000 respondents, 67 per cent discussed the level of crime very or fairly often, and 54 per cent the sentencing of criminals. Inflation (49 per cent) and the National Health Service (45 per cent) came third and fourth. The survey then went on to probe attitudes more deeply. Its authors were not optimistic, given their knowledge of public opinion on the subject as revealed in Gallup Polls. These revealed, for example, that 60 per cent of the population in 1982 were in favour of bringing back the cat, and 62 per cent birching, and that throughout the 1980s over 70 per cent (as against a pre-war figure of 55 per cent) were in favour of capital punishment. The more detailed survey, however, found a more complex set of reactions. Respondents were in favour of severe sentences for serious crimes, such as rape, mugging, and (less strongly) burglary. They also tended to see punishment in retributory terms: asked about the aims of sentencing for crimes like burglary or robbery, 44 per cent thought these included giving the offender 'what he deserves', 33 per cent thought the sentence should deter the offender from further crime, 17 per cent thought that it should deter others, and 28 per cent thought that it should reform the offender. The survey showed, on the other hand, a much greater flexibility of attitudes to less serious crime, and a lack of consistency between general attitudes and reactions to specific examples of sentencing.[45]

More surveys of this type are needed if we are to get a clearer insight into public attitudes to judicial punishment. In the interim, however, there is clearly a need for continued informed debate. But there remains a major obstacle to this: the difficulty of gaining access to information about punishment. If John Howard were alive today he would find much to write about in the prisons of England and Wales: it is, however, extremely unlikely that the Home Office would allow him through the gates of any of them (indeed, the ease of access which Howard was allowed when pursuing his investigations in prisons and cognate institutions both in Britain and abroad is, to the modern reader, one of the more remarkable features of his writings). The Official Secrets Act has, since the 1920s, obstructed investigation of what happens in prisons. As what we know of riots, the suppression of riots, and the occasional suspicious death of a prisoner indicates, there are perhaps things going on in prisons which the public might want to know about (e.g. Coggan and Walker, 1982). Similarly, the increased use of drugs and various forms of therapy in the treatment of offenders has its potentially sinister side, although as yet the moral issues here have been most vividly set out by a novelist.[46]

It is difficult, therefore, not to end on a gloomy note. Despite the existence of a state apparatus whose size and powers would have horrified our eighteenth-century forebears, it is seemingly impossible to perform what has long been seen as one of the major functions of the state, the protection of its citizens against criminals. The fullest recent survey of attitudes to crime in England, that carried out in Islington, noted that crime and vandalism were seen as social problems second only to unemployment in their seriousness, and on a par with poor housing and poor youth and children's facilities. Its authors noted:

> The impact of crime is considerable and it is a far from rare event. 31% of households in Islington had a serious crime committed against them in the last year – and it shapes their lives. For example, over a quarter of all people in Islington always avoid going out after dark because of fear of crime.[47]

One is left with a sorry feeling that whatever is done to such offenders as are caught will do little to alter this situation within our current system of punishment. For limited periods, and in limited cases (possibly England and Wales between the late nineteenth century and 1945 is an example), an effective and respected punishment system can have a role in helping keep down levels of crime. But as this book has suggested, the clearest message that the history of judicial punishment provides in general is that changes in the system or severity of punishment, whether in the sixteenth century or the late twentieth, rarely do much to alter the extent of criminality.

V

Conclusion

And so we find ourselves in our current situation, worried about crime, wondering what to do about it, struck constantly by indications that there are problems with our current system of punishment, struck also by indications that there are still flickers of imaginativeness in some of the remedies being proposed. As ever, our attention is focused on problems in our prisons: early 1988 saw reports that prisons may act as the great transmission belt by which AIDS will be spread into the general population; reports of riots, escapes, hostage-taking, overcrowding and of drug taking and alcohol-brewing among prisoners were more or less constant; old army or air force camps were taken over to be used as prisons; numerous remand prisoners were held in police cells; and industrial action among prison officers, including women officers at Holloway, continued. Against this familiar scenario of chaos were set some new ideas. The possibility of the privatization of part of the prison service, already a reality in the United States, was discussed. More commonly, variations were played on the theme, familiar for over a century, of how to keep offenders out of prison. The most discussed of these (and again something which has been tried in the United States) was the electronic tagging of offenders, who would thus be able to serve their 'sentence' in the community. There have also been suggestions for non-custodial sentences, involving curfews and work, for young offenders. Regular perusal of the newspapers convinces any reader that the question of how to punish or otherwise deal with criminals is an urgent social problem and a regular matter of social debate.

Faced with such urgent social issues, the natural reaction of historians is to feel diffident about the significance of what their discipline has to offer. Obviously, history offers no easy answers or recipes for panaceas: the crime control problems which we are currently facing, it might be argued, are so unique as to be without precedent. Moreover, as we have seen, the wide variety of measures tried in the past generally had little effect on levels of crime: indeed, one possible conclusion to be drawn from the study of the history of judicial punishment is that whatever is tried by way of punishment, it is extremely unlikely that levels of crime will be diminished. Similarly, many punishment strategies used in the past are no longer applicable: transportation is no longer an option, while it is likely that a return to a legal code which includes the possibility of the death penalty for petty property offences would not be acceptable.

Conversely, the very fact that previous generations have confronted crime and come to grips with it can be instructive, while the very diversity of past penal practices might offer solace as we continue with our own penal experiments. Study of the history of punishment can also help us understand our current situation, help us grasp something of why it is we have the penal institutions and the attitudes towards punishment which we have. It can also help shatter myths: above all, any notion of some past age when punishment 'worked'. And, connected with this ability to challenge myths, comes what is perhaps the most important quality which the history of punishment brings to current debate: the honing of an informed and intelligent scepticism about many of the arguments which are currently being deployed and many of the measures which are currently being suggested.

A second major contribution which the history of judicial punishment can make is to remind us that many of the specific issues which we are currently debating are not new. As J. E. Thomas has pointed out:

> An awareness of important events in penal history does more than simply make the present system intelligible. It demonstrates that many of the debates that we regard as peculiar to our age are, in fact, timeless and universal.[1]

Although an awareness of historical specificity and context ought to make us wary of claims for the 'timeless and universal', the continuities in attitudes to punishment and, to a lesser extent, penal practices, are striking. Sometimes this can be illustrated by specific examples: thus, as we have noted, although it has in practice been abolished, the arguments surrounding the death penalty for murder have remained largely unchanged between the 1860s and the present day. Similarly arguments surrounding the effectiveness of the prison are long established. Almost from the inception of the penitentiary prison, commentators were deploying the less-eligibility argument, and any attempt to ameliorate conditions for prisoners might be greeted by the comment that they were receiving better treatment than the poor outside the prison walls, and that committing crime was therefore a passport to an easy way of life. This sort of argument is still being deployed: it is noteworthy that one of the main areas of agreement between prison officers and prisoners today is that most people do not know what goes on inside prison, and are unwilling to stretch their imaginations to remedy this situation. Other, broader constants might be traced. The idea that sending people to prison is more likely to corrupt them than do anything else to them has been present from at least the early seventeenth century.[2] And the strategy of keeping young offenders away from hardened criminals, in hopes of preserving them from contamination, is still as much a part of the penal agenda as it was two centuries ago. We seem to rediscover these and other problems every five years or so, apparently unaware that they have been identified before.

Our study of the history of punishment leads us to two further considerations, connected to those which we have noted in the previous paragraph: the seemingly immovable nature of our current system of punishments; and the apparent impossibility of finding any political solution which would alter things for the better. The first of these points has frequently been raised by penologists: thus Peter Nokes has commented that 'people continue to be sent to prison at least partly because prisons are seen as the obvious places for them to be sent.'[3] In other words, prisons (and many of the other elements of our system of punishing and treating crime) are there because they're there: and attempts to suggest that this situation is in need of critical scrutiny, and is capable of being changed for the better, now as at so many points in the past, are usually met with indifference, incredulity, or mockery. Politicians, locked as they are into this paradigm, are clearly in no position to do much about using punishment to solve the 'crime problem'. Arguably, as we suggested at the end of the previous chapter, it is a problem which is probably incapable of being 'solved' within our current set of social arrangements anyway. But politicians, especially Home Secretaries and Prime Ministers (or would-be Prime Ministers) immediately before general elections, have to *sound* as if they can offer solutions, since they are aware that the public (again, as so often in the past) are, understandably, worried about crime and want something done about it. Unfortunately the public's attitudes are usually based on gut reactions, received wisdom, and their interpretation of what is put before them in their newspapers: sadly but inevitably, Everyman is not a John Howard or a Cesare Beccaria, nor Everywoman an Elizabeth Fry. The public wants reassurance that practices they understand will continue to be applied, normally more rigorously, and that the treatment models favoured by do-gooders be rejected as being too soft. Politicians, ever conscious of the need to give people what they want, are thus unlikely to engineer real penal reform. And, in any case, such interest groups as the Home Office or the Prison Officers' Association would be likely to deflect any such political initiative.

Perhaps the basic myth which needs to be attacked is the notion that punishment, or fear of punishment, will stop people from committing crimes. Obviously, as we have argued, it is one of a number of factors which keeps those of us who are not criminals on the right side of the law. Conversely, in any historical period, it is possible to find plenty of people whom fear of punishment did not deter and who (in so far as we can reconstruct recidivism) were not deterred or reformed by the experience of punishment. Over the centuries we have tried putting convicted offenders in the pillory in the market square, hanging them in large numbers, sending 30,000 of them to the American colonies and 160,000 of them to Australia, whipping them, putting them in hulks, putting them in solitary confinement in Pentonville, setting them on the treadwheel in Victorian local prisons, putting them in borstal, putting them on probation, fining them, giving them suspended sentences and making them perform Community Service Orders.

Crime, of course, is a constantly changing phenomenon, but whatever its mutations it is still with us, and all our varied expedients seem unable to stop it. This does not however stop us from trying, nor from accepting the rhetoric when new answers are discovered. An excellent, recent, and instructive illustration of this point was provided by the 1979 election campaign. Many will recall how during that campaign the Conservative Party envisaged one solution to the crime problem as the delivering of a 'short sharp shock' to young offenders. The idea was a straightforward one, struck a basic retributionist nerve and, summed up as it was in three alliterative monosyllables, was pitched at a level of complexity which the electorate could grasp. It received tremendous publicity, and in October 1979 William Whitelaw announced that the new experimental regime was to be introduced in two detention centres. Rather less publicity was given to the Home Office Young Offender Psychology Unit Report of 1984, *Tougher Regimes in Detention Centres*. This found that the new regime had 'no discernible effect on the rate at which trainees were reconvicted'. It was extended to all detention centres in England and Wales on 6 March 1985, despite this official announcement of its ineffectiveness.[4] The stage management of the introduction of a penal policy is evidently now more important than its actual usefulness.

An historical perspective on these matters can be provided by the two periods within the time span covered by this book which seem to have experienced a fall in levels of prosecuted crime. The first of these set in over the second half of the seventeenth century, the second at the end of the nineteenth. Neither of these, it will be remembered, can be attributed to the implementation of punishment. The first was largely due to the easing of pressure at the base of society (and a concomitant easing of official fears) when a century of demographic growth came to an end, the population stabilized, and the economy caught up with the demands which society made upon it.[5] The second was in some respects similar. Some contemporaries, indeed, did connect the fall in levels of indicted crime to the prison system's effectiveness. But the best modern opinion puts it down to a complexity of factors: better policing, better living standards among the working class, in fact a general settling down of society after a period of industrialization and urbanization.[6] One is tempted to predict that if crime rates fall in the immediate future, it will be the outcome not of initiatives in how crime is punished, but rather the simple demographic fact that there will be fewer teenagers about. This means that there will be less juvenile crime and thus, in the fullness of time, a diminution in the number of adult offenders.

Study of the history of punishment also engenders suspicion about any attempt to relate changes in penal policy to any total or deterministic theories of social change. Detailed study of the early modern period reveals a complex pattern of punishments which casts doubts on Foucault's model. The realities of Victorian prison life and detailed examination of how Victorian penal policy was framed makes it difficult to accept any simplistic connections between the rise of the penitentiary prison and the rise of capitalism. What the period 1780–1850 – seen by both Marxists and Foucault as the decisive one – actually reveals is a complicated situation in which a number of varied and to some extent contradictory factors were in operation. Thus the history of tranportation shows a government frantically scrabbling to continue implementing a penal policy because nothing better could be thought of; the use of the hulks shows how a temporary penal expedient could last for decades; the story of the prison, in general terms, shows how an innovation can quickly be accepted as part of normality; while the history of the penitentiary prison is a sad example of how an innovation meant to be of benefit both to society and to the individual being punished can quickly go stale. Fitting all of these into a deterministic model of change proves troublesome. They do, however, provide instructive historical parallels for some of our current attempts to devise useful forms of punishment.

Another model for explaining changes in modes of punishment has recently been suggested by Pieter Spierenburg.[7] Like many Dutch scholars, he has been influenced by the writings of the sociologist Norbert Elias (notably 1982). Concentrating on the early modern period, and consciously offering a rival interpretation to Foucault's, Spierenburg constructs a model of social change based on economic change, yet essentially different from the Marxist model in its concentration on ideology and its emphasis on the quasi-autonomous role of the state. Though stimulating and benefiting from being founded on extensive empirical research, Spierenburg's model has its drawbacks. Explaining change in judicial punishments through changing sensibilities is all very well, but there is still the problem of why it is that sensibilities change. Nevertheless, Spierenburg's work is valuable on two levels. Firstly, it provides yet another reminder of the uselessness of any 'transition from barbarism' model: Spierenburg's work reinforces our basic contention that past punishments, however unpleasant they may seem to the modern observer, had their own rationale. And, secondly, it reminds us of the possibilities of constructing other models of long-term change in penal policy, and the connection of such changes with broader socio-economic developments, than those offered by crude Marxism. The English historical tradition is cautious of grand theory, but there is surely considerable virtue in attempting to place our growing store of empirically based historical studies against wider paradigms of change: against those provided by a more sophisticated Marxism, perhaps, or by Max Weber.

Such a contention, of course, locates the problem of the history of crime at a fairly high level of abstraction. Yet for most people in the past, as for most of us today, worry over crime, and hence by extension punishment, operated on a rather more immediate level. Currently, our main concern is how likely we are to be mugged, burgled, raped or assaulted, and whether the areas in which we live are likely to become more dangerous and less pleasant. 'Community', despite being a term which defies precise definition, is one which is much used currently, a symptom of a desire for some idealized form of human relationships rather than a reflection of the widespread importance of 'the community' in reality. Yet we must reiterate that one dimension of crime control problems is the degree to which we feel safe in our immediate environment: the current emphasis on 'community' aspects of crime prevention and policing is one aspect of this. Possibly, some elements of punishment might be adjusted to this strand in current thinking. As we have noted, part of the approbation given to Community Service Orders derives from the way in which the offender undergoing punishment is seen to do so, and is often thought to be doing something useful in the community. There are, perhaps, other ways in which community values might be extended into punishment: as an extreme, for example, it is possible to envisage something like the pre-industrial shaming punishment, with those convicted for certain offences having their delinquencies publicized on local television and radio.

Overall, therefore, the study of the history of judicial punishment throws considerable light on our current situation, both in demonstrating continuities and recurrent problems, and in demonstrating those areas where historical contexts are entirely different. Two final points need to be made. The first is, assuming that our society remains more or less as it is, that we, like our ancestors, will continue to need some system of judicial punishment. Whatever the deficiencies of our present system, it at least peforms some function in combating crime. However uncomfortable the process might be for the individual offender, judicial punishment is less socially disruptive than would be a return to the feud as a means of settling criminal disputes. The second is to return to the thought that the most important function of judicial punishment is to induce a feeling of security and well-being among those who are not criminals. In making this statement it is not my purpose to disparage the efforts made by policemen, judges, prison staff, social workers, probation officers, and others involved in the punishment and treatment of criminals. But, in the last resort, we punish criminals because to do so makes us feel securer, and reassures us through the reassertion of social values, rather than because we have any well founded hopes that so doing will either make the individual offender desist from offending again, or achieve a more general lowering of levels of crime.

Notes

I. Introduction

1 The figures are based on: *Home Office: Criminal Statistics England and Wales 1986*; *Home Office: Prison Statistics for England and Wales 1986;* and *Report of the Work of the Prison Service 1986–87*. These reports are published annually, and follow the earlier Reports (stretching back into the nineteenth century) of the Directors of Convict Prisons, Commissioners of Prisons, Commissioners of Prisons and Directors of Convict Prisons, and of the Prison Department in forming the basis for the discussion of statistical and other trends in punishment. Unless otherwise stated, figures related to imprisonment given in the text are based upon the then existing body's report for that year.
2 Harrison and Gretton, 1986, p. 20.
3 Shaw, 1980.
4 Lenman and Parker, 1980; Soman, 1980.
5 Gluckman, 1965; Moore, 1978; Roberts, 1979.
6 There is an extensive literature relating to theories of punishment, and an exhaustive bibliography cannot be given here. Moberley, 1968, is a classic, while Grupp, 1971, is a reader which is useful in demonstrating the variety of approaches involved in the subject. These can be explored further in Klare, 1966; Zimring and Hawkins, 1973; Andenaes, 1974; von Hirsch, 1976; Riedel and Vales, 1977; Walker, 1980; and Bean, 1981.
7 Sharpe, 1984, p. 174.
8 Moberley, 1968, p. 269.
9 Cited in Grupp, 1971, p. 11.
10 Ibid., p. 15.
11 Hay, 1975.
12 Radzinowicz and Hood, 1986, p. 774.
13 Langbein, 1983.

II. The Old Penal Regime

1 Ingram, 1984.
2 Sharpe, 1983, p. 149.
3 Hamilton, 1878, p. 85.
4 Fletcher and Stevenson, 1985.
5 Spargo, 1944.
6 Ratcliffe, Johnson and Williams, 1935–64, vol. 7, p. 148; Sharpe, 1983, p. 149.
7 J. S. Cockburn (ed.), *Calendar of Assize Records: Kent Indictments Elizabeth I*, HMSO, London, 1979, p. 440; *Calendar of Assize Records: Essex Indictments Elizabeth I*, HMSO, London, 1978, p. 191. Cockburn's *Calendar* of the Home Circuit of the Assizes, published between 1975 and 1985, will give the student ready access to one of the few archival series giving evidence of the punishment of serious crime in this period. His *Introduction* volume of 1985 contains a good discussion of sentencing, and some useful statistical tables. The only comparable source to be examined are the archives of the Court of Great Sessions of the Palatinate of Cheshire, notably the Crown Books (Public Records Office, CHES 21/1–5). Comparable records survive for a number of Welsh counties, but these have yet to be studied.
8 Jeaffreson, 1886–92, vol. 1, pp. 1, 95, 114, 189, 234; cf. Ingram, 1984.
9 Ingram, 1987.
10 Sharpe, 1983, p. 94.
11 Ibid., p. 119.
12 Ibid., p. 158.
13 Ratcliff, Johnson and Williams, 1935–64, vol. 1, p. 2.
14 Innes, 1980.
15 Bellamy, 1973, p. 157; Hanawalt, 1979, pp. 57–9.
16 These findings are based on a preliminary survey of the Palatinate of Lancaster Clerk of the Crown Assize Rolls (P.L. 25) and Indictments (P.L. 26). Documents consulted were: Public Record Office, P.L. 25/5–7; 25/11; 25/14; 25/22–24; 26/14/1; 26/296/3; 26/296/4.
17 Sharpe, 1984, pp. 64–5.
18 Ibid., 1983, p. 183; PRO, CHES, 25/1–5.
19 Hay *et al.*, 1975, p. 13.
20 Sharpe, 1985.
21 Goodcole, 1618, Sig. A4.
22 Sharpe, 1985.
23 Cited in Breward, 1969, pp. 17–18.
24 Thoresby, 1830, vol. 1, p. 131.
25 Rosen, 1969, p. 167.
26 Veall, 1970.

27 e.g. Soman, 1980.
28 Prest, 1986; Brooks, 1986.
29 Shapiro, 1983.
30 Radzinowicz, 1948, p. 147, 159.
31 Beattie, 1986.
32 Anon, 1701.
33 Paley, 1838, vol. 2, pp. 424–5.
34 e.g. Langbein, 1983; King, 1984.
35 Samaha, 1978.
36 King, 1983; Beattie, 1986, pp. 213–35.
37 Beattie, 1986, pp. 450–1.
38 Cockburn, 1985, 117–21.
39 Bellamy, 1984, pp. 156–8; Sharpe, 1983, p. 145.
40 Cockburn, 1985, pp. 121–3.
41 e.g. Babington, 1677, pp. 55–6.
42 Beattie, 1986, p. 473.
43 Ekirch, 1987.
44 Beattie, 1986, p. 507.
45 Evans, 1882.
46 Beattie, 1986, pp. 553, 554.
47 Cited in Radzinowicz, 1948, p. 485.
48 Radzinowicz, 1948, pp. 153–5; Hamilton, 1878, p. 131.
49 Radzinowicz, 1948, pp. 574–6.

III. The Nineteenth Century

1 e.g. Rusche and Kirchheimer, 1939; Melossi and Pavarini, 1981.
2 Beattie, 1986, p. 576.
3 Branch Johnson, 1970, p. 34.
4 Ibid., p. 43.
5 Ibid., p. 33.
6 Ibid., p. 18.
7 Hughes, 1987, is a good survey accessible to the general reader, and has a useful bibliography. It should, however, be read in conjunction with Shaw, 1966, and Radzinowicz and Hood, 1986, ch. 14.
8 Radzinowicz and Hood, 1986, p. 138.
9 Ibid., p. 477.
10 Hughes, 1987, p. 493.
11 The literature on the rise of the prison is enormous. Many readers will enter the subject through reading Foucault, 1977. This work has received considerable criticism, one of the most useful critiques for those working from an historical perspective being Garland, 1986. Ignatieff, 1978, has also proved influential, while Evans, 1982, offers a

fascinating insight into early prison design, a theme taken into the twentieth century by Dickens, McConville and Fairweather, 1978. McConville, 1981, is a solid empirical study, Freeman, 1978, is a useful if sometimes patchy collection of essays, while Thomas (1972) and Priestley (1985) provide sympathetic accounts of the uniformed staff and of prisoners respectively. Those with a taste for original materials might read Mayhew and Binney, 1862, while Howard, 1777, is a classic. Studies of foreign developments include: Perrot, 1980; Walker, 1980; Rothman, 1971; O'Brien, 1982; Petit, 1984; Spierenburg, 1984a, 1984b, and 1986–7. Rusche and Kirchheimer, 1939, is an important pioneering attempt to grapple with long-term change, a more recent work of this type being Melossi and Pavarini, 1981.

12 Ignatieff, 1978, p. 3.
13 See Emsley, 1987, pp. 29–36 for statistics.
14 Ignatieff, 1978, p. 210.
15 S. and B. Webbs' *English Prisons under Local Government* (1922) is a richly detailed account of local prisons though more recently de Lacy (1986) has demonstrated admirably how a local approach to prison history can help modify grand theory about punishment and provides (pp. 231–2) a useful note of other local studies in print. Two of the more useful of these are Stockdale, 1977, and Saunders, 1986.
16 McConville, 1981, p. 222.
17 Cited in Ignatieff, 1978, p. 32.
18 Innes, 1980.
19 Foucault, 1977.
20 Priestley, 1985.
21 Cited in ibid., p. 22.
22 Cited in ibid., p. 43.
23 Ibid., p. 123.
24 Thomas, 1972.
25 As the reader will notice, this section depends heavily on Radzinowicz and Hood, 1986, an excellent and detailed account of developments within the period with an exhaustive bibliography for those wishing to take matters further. Garland, 1986, provides a well-focused and scholarly account of developments *c.* 1895–1914, again with a good bibliography, while Harding, 1988, offers an original interpretation of the origins of the Gladstone Committee.
26 Emsley, 1987, pp. 223, 230.
27 Bcattic, 1986, pp. 82–5.
28 Radzinowicz and Hood, 1986, pp. 661–88.
29 Dinwiddy, 1982.
30 Davies, 1980.
31 Radzinowicz and Hood, 1986, pp. 689–96.

32 Ibid., pp. 699–708.
33 Ibid., pp. 709–11.
34 Ibid., pp. 711–19.
35 Gillis, 1975.
36 e.g., Walvin, 1982.
37 Radzinowicz and Hood, 1986, p. 174.
38 Ibid., p. 224.
39 Ibid., pp. 633–48.
40 Emsley, 1987, pp. 234–5.
41 Philips, 1977, pp. 179, 222, 224, 227.
42 These figures are drawn from a printed schedule headed *West Riding Prison Wakefield. Offences of Prisoners Committed convicted during the Quarter ending 30th September, 1877*, which is bound in the '1881–82, 1877' volume of an eight volume set entitled *Wakefield Calendar of All the Prisoners*, J. B. Morrell Library, University of York, class number Q 42.74 WAK. This set consists of bound calendars, etc, from Wakefield prison for the period 1848–82. The calendars are unedited and lack through pagination, but contain a mass of detail about those entering a local prison during the period they cover.
43 Radzinowicz and Hood, 1986, pp. 618–24, 777.
44 Ibid., pp. 603–17; Priestley, 1985, pp. 283, 286.
45 Gatrell, 1980; Radzinowicz and Hood, 1986, pp. 113–23; Emsley, 1987, pp. 35, 42.
46 de Lacey, 1986, p. 3.
47 Garland, 1985, p. 847.

IV. The Twentieth Century

1 Garland, 1985.
2 Ruggles-Brise, 1921; *Dictionary of National Biography* (*DNB*).
3 *DNB*; Ruck, 1951.
4 Hobhouse and Brockway, 1922, pp. 3–4.
5 For prisons during this period, see Ruggles-Brise, 1921; Hobhouse and Brockway, 1922; Rhodes, 1933; Ruck, 1951; and Thomas, 1972. Clemmer, 1940 is, as suggested in the text, a classic of sociological research. For the broader dimensions of a vital aspect of punishment and treatment during this period, see Bailey, 1987.
6 Jones, Cornes and Stockford, 1977.
7 Cited in ibid., p. 9.
8 Hood, 1965; Radzinowicz and Hood, 1986, pp. 384–97; Hobhouse and Brockway, 1922, pp. 410–40.
9 Hood, 1965, p. 15.
10 Ibid., p. 54.

11 Ibid., pp. 106–7.
12 Ibid., p. 111.
13 Jones, 1962, p. 163; Hobhouse and Brockway, 1922, pp. 441–66.
14 Garland, 1985; Harding, 1988.
15 Radzinowicz and Hood, 1986, p. 777.
16 Joan King, 1969, pp. 1–5.
17 J. E. Thomas, 1972.
18 Ibid. p. 171.
19 Rhodes, 1933.
20 J. E. Thomas, 1972, pp. 157–9.
21 Amnesty International, 1979, p. 17.
22 The debate on capital punishment has attracted a large literature, some of the more substantial items being the reports of Royal Commissions and other official bodies. Some of the flavour of the twentieth-century debate can be gleaned from: Calvert, 1927; Gardiner, 1956; Tuttle, 1961; Christoph, 1962; and from reading the appropriate sections of *Hansard*.
23 Calvert, 1927, pp. 45–90.
24 Cited in Tuttle, 1961, p. 21.
25 Ibid., p. 22.
26 Ibid., p. 42.
27 Ibid., p. 108.
28 Christoph, 1962, p. 171.
29 The post-1945 prison system is another subject about which a great deal has been written. Two recent works, written from an intelligently critical position, are Fitzgerald and Sim, 1982, and Stern, 1987. Objectives and developments over the past forty years can be followed in: Fox, 1952; HMSO, 1959; HMSO, 1966; HMSO, 1969; Sparks, 1971; and Hall Williams, 1975. Good studies of individual prisons are provided by Morris, Morris and Baker, 1963, and King and Elliott, 1977. Thomas, 1972, presents a sympathetic view of the situation from the prison officers' point of view.
30 *New Society*, 1985, pp. 367–8.
31 Biles, 1983.
32 King and Elliott, 1977, p. 8.
33 Fitzgerald and Sim, 1982, p. 27.
34 King and Elliott, 1977; Stern, 1987, pp. 142–3.
35 Stern, 1987, p. 77.
36 Pitts, 1988.
37 Walker, Farrington and Tucker, 1981; Stanley and Baginsky, 1984, ch. 4.
38 Stanley and Baginsky, 1984, pp. 76–81.
39 Walker, Farrington and Tucker, 1981, p. 359.
40 HMSO, 1975; ibid., 1977; Young, 1979; Vass, 1986.

41 Dunlop and McCabe, 1965, p. 10.
42 Burney, 1985.
43 Ibid., pp. 4–5.
44 e.g. HMSO, 1969; Walker, 1969; Devlin, 1970; Thomas, 1970.
45 Walker, Hough and Lewis, 1988.
46 Burgess, 1962.
47 Jones, MacLean and Young, 1986, p. 201.

V. Conclusion

1 Cited in Blom-Cooper, 1974, p. 54.
2 Sharpe, 1984, p. 182.
3 Blom-Cooper, 1974, p. 75.
4 Pitts, 1988, pp. 51–2.
5 Sharpe, 1984.
6 Gatrell, 1980.
7 Spierenburg, 1984a.

Bibliography

Amnesty International, *The Death Penalty: Amnesty International Report*, London, 1979

Andenaes, Johanness, *Punishment and Deterrence*, Ann Arbor, 1974

Anon, *Hanging not Punishment enough for Murtherers, Highway Men, and House Breakers, etc.*, London, 1701

Babington, Zachary, *Advice to Grand Jurors in Cases of Blood*, London, 1677

Bailey, Victor, *Delinquency and Citizenship: Reclaiming the Young Offender, 1914–1948*, Oxford, 1987

Bean, Philip, *Punishment: a Philosophical and Criminological Enquiry*, Oxford, 1981

Beattie, John, *Crime and the Courts in England 1660–1800*, Oxford, 1986

Beccaria, Cesare, *An Essay on Crimes and Punishments*, London, 1767

Bellamy, John, *Crime and Public Order in England in the later Middle Ages*, London, 1973

——, *Criminal Law and Society in Late Medieval and Tudor England*

Biles, David, 'Crime and Imprisonment: a two-decade Comparison between England and Wales and Australia', *British Journal of Criminology*, 23, 1983

Blom-Cooper, Louis, ed., *Progress in Penal Reform*, Oxford, 1974

Branch Johnson, W., *The English Prison Hulks*, London, 1957

Breward, Ian, ed., *William Perkins*, Abingdon, 1969

Brooks, C. W., *Pettyfoggers and Vipers of the Commonwealth: The 'Lower Branch' of the Legal Profession in Early Modern England*, Cambridge, 1986

Burgess, Anthony, *A Clockwork Orange*, London, 1962

Burney, Elizabeth, *Sentencing Young People: what went wrong with the Criminal Justice Act 1982*, Aldershot and Brookfield, Vermont, 1985

Calvert, E. Roy, *Capital Punishment in the Twentieth Century*, London and New York, 1927

Christoph, James B., *Capital Punishment and British Politics: the British Movement to Abolish the Death Penalty 1945–57*, London, 1962

Clemmer, Donald, *The Prison Community*, 1940: reprinted, New York etc., 1958

Cobley, John, *The Origins of the First Fleet Convicts*, Sydney, 1970
Cockburn, J. S., *Introduction*, to J. S. Cockburn, ed., *A Calendar of Assize Records*, London, 1985
Coggan, Geoff and Walker, Martin, *Frightened for my Life: an Account of Deaths in British Prisons*, London, 1982
Davis, Jennifer, 'The London Garrotting Panic of 1862. A Moral Panic and the Creation of a Criminal Class in mid-Victorian England', in Gatrell, V. A. C., Lenman, Bruce and Parker, Geoffrey, eds., *Crime and the Law: the Social History of Crime in Western Europe since 1500*, London, 1980
de Lacy, Margaret, *Prison Reform in Lancashire, 1700–1850: A Study in Local Administration*, Manchester, 1986 (Chetham Society), 3rd Series, 33
Devlin, Keith, *Sentencing Offenders in Magistrates' Courts*, London, 1970
Dickens, Peter, McConville, Sean and Fairweather, Leslie, eds., *Penal Policy and Prison Architecture: Selected Papers from a Symposium held at the University of Sussex in July 1977*, Cheshire, 1978
Dictionary of National Biography
Dinwiddy, J. R., 'The early nineteenth-century Campaign to end Flogging in the Army', *English Historical Review*, 97, 1982
Dodge, Calvert R., *A World without Prisons: Alternatives to Incarceration throughout the World*, Lexington, Mass., and Toronto, 1979
Dunlop, Anne B. and McCabe, Sarah, *Young Men in Detention Centres*, London and New York, 1965
Ekirch, A. Roger, *Bound for America: The Transportation of British Convicts to the Colonies*, 1718–1775, Oxford, 1987
Elias, Norbert, *The Civilizing Process: State Formation and Civilization*, Oxford, 1982
Emsley, Clive, *Crime and Society in England 1750–1900*, London, 1987
Evans, Robin, *The Fabrication of Virtue: English Prison Architecture, 1750–1840*, Cambridge, 1982
Fitzgerald, Mike and Sim, Joe, *British Prisons*, 2nd edn, Oxford, 1982
Fletcher, Anthony and Stevenson, John, eds., *Order and Disorder in Early Modern England*, Cambridge, 1985
Foucault, Michel, *Discipline and Punish: the Birth of the Prison*, London, 1977
Fox, L. W., *The English Prison and Borstal System*, London, 1952
Freeman, John, ed., *Prisons Past and Future*, London, 1978
Gardiner, G. A. G., *Capital Punishment as a Deterrent: and the Alternatives*, London, 1956
Garland, David, *Punishment and Welfare: a History of Penal Strategies*, Aldershot, 1985
——, 'Review Essay: Foucault's Discipline and Punish: An Exposition and Critique', *American Bar Foundation Research Journal*, Fall, 1986
Gatrell, V. A. C., 'The Decline of Theft and Violence in Victorian and Edwardian England', in Gatrell, V. A. C., Lenman, Bruce and Parker,

Geoffrey, eds., *Crime and the Law: the Social History of Crime since 1500*, London, 1980
Gillis, John R., 'The Evolution of Juvenile Delinquency in England 1890–1914', *Past and Present*, 67, 1975
Gluckman, Max, *Politics, Law and Ritual in Tribal Society*, Oxford, 1965
Goodcole, Henry, *A True Declaration of the Happy Conversion, Contrition and Christian Preparation of Francis Robinson, Gentleman, who for Counterfeiting the Great Seale of England was Drawen, Hang'd and Quartered at Charing Cross, on Friday Last, being the Twentieth Day of November 1618*, London, 1618
Grupp, Stanley E., ed., *Theories of Punishment*, Bloomington and London, 1971
Hall Williams, J. E., *Changing Prisons*, London, 1975
Hamilton, A. H. A., *Quarter Sessions from Queen Elizabeth to Queen Anne*, London, 1878
Hanawalt, Barbara A., *Crime and Conflict in English Communities 1300–1348*, Cambridge, Mass., and London, 1979
Harding, Christopher, 'The Inevitable End of a Discredited System?: the Origins of the Gladstone Committee Report on Prisons, 1895', *The Historical Journal*, 31, 1988
Harrison, Anthony and Gretton, John, eds., *Crime U.K. 1986: an Economic, Social and Policy Audit*, Newbury, 1986
Hay, Douglas, 'Property, Authority and the Criminal Law', in Douglas Hay, et al., *Albion's Fatal Tree: Crime and Society in Eighteenth-Century England*, London, 1975
HMSO, *Penal Practice in a Changing Society*, London, 1959
——, *The Child, the Family and the Young Offender*, London, 1965
——, *Report of the Inquiry into Prison Escapes and Security by Admiral of the Fleet, the Earl Mountbatten of Burma*, London, 1966
——, *Children in Trouble*, 1968
——, *People in Prison in England and Wales*, London, 1969
——, *The Sentence of the Court: A Handbook for Courts in the Treatment of Offenders*, London, 1969b
——, *Community Service Orders: A Home Office Research Unit Report*, Home Office Research Studies, 29, London, 1975
——, *The Community Service Order Assessed in 1976*, Home Office Research Study, 39, London, 1977
Hobhouse, Stephen and Brockway, A. Fenner, *English Prisons Today: Being the Report of the Prison System Enquiry Committee*, London, 1922
Hood, Roger, *Borstal Re-assessed*, London, 1965
Howard, John, *The State of the Prisons in England and Wales, with Preliminary Observations and an Account of some Foreign Prisons*, Warrington, 1777

Hughes, Robert, *The Fatal Shore: A History of the Transportation of Convicts to Australia, 1787–1868*, London, 1987

Ignatieff, Michael, *A Just Measure of Pain: The Penitentiary in the Industrial Revolution 1750–1850*, New York, 1978

Ingram, Martin, 'Ridings, Rough Music and the "Reform of Popular Culture" in Early Modern England', *Past and Present*, 105, 1984

——, *Church Courts, Sex and Marriage in England, 1570–1640*, Cambridge, 1987

Innes, Joanna, 'The King's Bench Prison in the later eighteenth century: Law, Authority and Order in a London Debtor's Prison', in John Brewer and John Styles, eds., *An Ungovernable people: the English and Their Law in the Seventeenth and Eighteenth Centuries*, London, 1980

——, 'Prisons for the Poor: English Bridewells 1550–1800', in Francis G. Snyder and Douglas Hay, eds., *Labour, Law and Crime*, London, 1987

Jeaffreson, J. C., ed., *Middlesex County Records*, Middlesex County Record Society, Clerkenwell, 1886–92

Jones, Howard, *Crime and the Penal System*, 2nd edn, 1962

Jones, Howard, Cornes, Paul and Stockford, Richard, *Open Prisons*, London, Henley and Boston, 1977

Jones, Trevor, MacLean, Brian and Young, Jock, *The Islington Crime Survey: Crime, Victimization and Policy in Inner-City London*, Aldershot, 1986

King, Joan, ed., *The Probation and After Care Service*, 3rd edn, London, 1969

King, Peter, 'Decision Makers and Decision Making in the English Criminal Law 1750–1800', *The Historical Journal*, 27, 1984

King, Roy D. and Elliott, Kenneth W., *Albany: Birth of a Prison: End of an Era*, London, 1977

Klare, Hugh J., ed., *Changing Concepts of Crime and its Treatment*, Oxford, 1966

Langbein, J. H., '*Albion's* Fatal Flaws', *Past and Present*, 98, 1983

Lenman, Bruce and Parker, Geoffrey, 'The State, the Community and the Criminal Law in Early Modern Europe', in Gatrell, V. A. C., Lenman, Bruce and Parker, Geoffrey, *Crime and the Law: the Social History of Crime in Western Europe since 1500*, London, 1980

Lewis, Frank D., 'The Cost of Convict Transportation from Britain to Australia, 1796–1810', *Economic History Review*, 2nd Series, 41, 1988

McConville, Sean, *A History of English Prison Administration*, vol. 1, London, 1981

Mayhew, Henry and Binny, John, *The Criminal Prisons of London, and Scenes of Prison Life*, 1862: reprinted London, 1968

Melossi, Dario and Pavarini, Massimo, *The Prison and the Factory: Origins of the Penitentiary System*, London and Basingstoke, 1981

Moberley, Sir Walter, *The Ethics of Punishment*, London, 1968

Moore, S. F., *Law as Process: an Anthropological Approach*, London, 1978

Morris, Terence, Morris, Pauline, and Baker, Barbara, *Pentonville: a Sociological Study of an English Prison*, London, 1963

O'Brien, Patricia, *The Promise of Punishment: Prisons in Nineteenth-Century France*, Princeton, 1982

Paley, William, *The Works of William Paley, DD*, ed., Paxton, J., London, 5 vols., 1838

Perrot, Michelle, ed., *L'Impossible Prison: Récherches sur le Système Pénitentiare au XIXe Siècle*, Paris, 1980

Petit, Jacques G., *La Prison, le Bagne et l'Histoire*, Geneva, 1984

Philips, David, *Crime and Authority in Victorian England*, London, 1977

Pitts, John, *The Politics of Juvenile Crime*, London, 1988

Pointing, John, ed., *Alternatives to Custody*, Oxford, 1986

Prest, Wilfrid R., *The Rise of the Barristers: a Social History of the English Bar 1590–1640*, Oxford, 1986

Priestley, Philip, *Victorian Prison Lives: English Prison Biography 1830–1914*, London, 1985

Radzinowicz, Leon, *A History of the English Criminal Law*, vol. 1, 'The Movement for Reform', London, 1948

Radzinowicz, Leon and Hood, Roger, *A History of English Criminal Law*, vol. 5., 'The Emergence of Penal Policy', 1986

Ratcliffe, S. C., Johnson, H. C. and Williams, N. J., *Warwick County Records*, Warwick, 8 vols., 1935–64

Rhodes, A. J., *Dartmoor Prison: A Record of 126 Years of Prisoner of War and Convict Life 1806–1932*, London, 1933

Riedel, Marc and Vales, Pedro A., eds., *Treating the Offender: Problems and Issues*, New York, Washington and London, 1977

Roberts, Simon, *Order and Dispute*, Harmondsworth, 1979

Rosen, Barbara, *Witchcraft*, London, 1969

Rothman, David J., *The Discovery of the Asylum: Social Order and Disorder in the New Republic*, Boston, 1971

Ruck, S. K., ed., *Paterson on Prisons*, London, 1951

Ruggles-Brise, Evelyn, *The English Prison System*, London, 1921

Rusche, Georg and Kirchheimer, Otto, *Punishment and Social Structure*, 1939: reprinted New York, 1967

Samaha, Joel, 'Hanging for Felony: the Rule of Law in Elizabethan Colchester', *The Historical Journal*, 21, 1978

Saunders, Janet, 'Warwickshire Magistrates and Prison Reform', *Midland History*, 11, 1986

Scull, Andrew, *Decarceration: Community Treatment and the Deviant – A Radical View*, 2nd edn, Oxford, 1984

Shapiro, Barbara, *Probability and Certainty in Seventeenth-Century England: a*

Study in the Relationships between Natural Science, History, Law and Literature, Princeton, 1983

Sharpe, J. A., *Crime in Seventeenth-Century England: a County Study*, Cambridge, 1983

——, *Crime in Early Modern England 1550–1750*, London, 1984

——, ' "Last Dying Speeches": Religion, Ideology and Public Execution in Seventeenth-Century England', *Past and Present*, 107, 1985

Shaw, A. G. L., *Convicts and the Colonies: a Study of Penal Transportation from Great Britain and Ireland to Australia and other Parts of the British Empire*, London, 1966

Shaw, Stephen, *Paying the Penalty: an Analysis of the Cost of Penal Sanctions*, London, 1980

Soman, A., 'Deviance and Criminal Justice in Western Europe 1300–1800: an Essay in Structure', *Criminal Justice History: an International Annual*, 1, 1980

Sparks, Richard F., *Local Prisons: the Crisis in the English Penal System*, London, 1971

Spargo, John Webster, *Juridicial Folklore in England, Illustrated by the Cucking-Stool*, Durham, North Carolina, 1944

Spierenburg, Pieter, *The Spectacle of Suffering: Execution and the Evolution of Repression: from a preindustrial Metropolis to the European Experience*, Cambridge, 1984a

——, *The Emergence of Carceral Institutions: Prisons, Galleys and Lunatic Asylums*, Rotterdam, 1984b

——, 'From Amsterdam to Auburn: an Explanation for the Rise of the Prison in Sixteenth-Century Holland and Nineteenth-Century America', *Journal of Social History*, 20, 1986–7

Stanley, Stephen and Baginsky, Mary, *Alternatives to Prison: an Examination of non-custodial Sentencing of Offenders*, London and Washington, 1984

Stern, Vivien, *Bricks of Shame: Britain's Prisons*, Harmondsworth, 1987

Stockdale, Eric, *A Study of Bedford Prison 1660–1877*, London, 1977

Thomas, D. A., *Principles of Sentencing: the Sentencing Policy of the Court of Appeal Criminal Division*, London, 1970

Thomas, J. E., *The English Prison Officer since 1850: a Study in Conflict*, London, 1972

Thoresby, Ralph, *The Diary of Ralph Thoresby*, ed. Joseph Hunter, 2 vols., 1830

Tuttle, E. A., *The Crusade against Capital Punishment*, Cambridge, 1961

van Dülmen, Richard, *Theater des Schreckens: Gerichspraxis und Strafrituale in der Frühen Neuzeit*, Munich, 2nd edn, 1986

Vass, Anthony, 'Community Service: Areas of Concern and Suggestions for Change', *The Howard Journal of Criminal Justice*, 25, 1986

Veall, D., *The Popular Movement for Law Reform 1640–1660*, Oxford, 1970 von Hirsch, Andrew, *Doing Justice: the Choice of Punishments*, New York, 1976

Walker, Nigel, *Sentencing in a Rational Society*, London, 1969

——, *Punishment, Danger and Stigma: the Morality of Criminal Justice*, Oxford, 1980

Walker, Nigel, Farrington, David P. and Tucker, Gillian, 'Reconviction Rates of Adult Males after Different Sentences', *British Journal of Criminology*, 21, 1981

Walker, Nigel, Hough, Mike and Lewis, Helen, 'Tolerance of Leniency and Severity in England and Wales', in Nigel Walker and Mike Hough, eds., *Public Attitudes to Sentencing: Surveys from five Countries*, Aldershot, 1988

Walker, Samuel, *Popular Justice: a History of American Criminal Justice*, New York and Oxford, 1980

Walvin, James, *A Child's World: A Social History of English Childhood*, 1982

Webb, Sidney and Beatrice, *English Prisons under Local Government*, 1922: reprinted London, 1963

Young, Warren, *Community Service Orders: the Development and Use of a New Penal Measure*, London, 1979

Zimring, Franklin E. and Hawkins, Gordon Jay, *Deterrence: the Legal Threat in Crime Control*, Chicago and London, 1973

Index

adultery, 20, 22
Albany prison, 111, 114
America: prison system, 64–5, 92–3; probation system, 81; transportation to, 43–4, 45, 49, 51; *see also* United States
Amnesty International, 100
Amsterdam, Rasp House, 62
apprentices, runaway, 26
Arthur, Sir George, 57
assault, 24, 83
Auburn prison system, 65
Australia, 54–61, 73, 110

Baginsky, Mary, 121
Bagthorpe institution, 95
banishment, 42
Banks, Joseph, 54
Beattie, John, 37, 52
Beccaria, Cesare, 6, 127
Bedford Prison, 94
Belgium, 102, 110, 121
Bellman, John, 22
Bentham, Jeremy, 62–3, 64, 68, 71, 86
Bentley, Derek, 106
Biggs, Ronald, 112
Birmingham prison, 112
Blake, George, 112
'Bloody Code', 30, 36, 38, 45, 47, 49, 50, 103
borstal system, 90, 93–6, 119, 127
Botany Bay, 54, 55–6
branding, 23, 40
branks, the, 19
Bridewell, 22, 25
Bright, John, 103
Brockway, A. Fenner, 90, 96
Brooke, Henry, 107
brothel-keeping, 21–2
Burghley, William Cecil, first Baron, 40
burning at the stake, 27
Bury St Edmunds gaol, 72

Calvert, E. Roy, 102, 104
Cambridge gaol, 33
Camp Hill, 95, 96
Campbell, Duncan, 52
capital punishment: abolition debates, 75–6, 100–8, 126; comparisons abroad, 102–3; eighteenth century, 36–9, 43–5; legislation, 46–7, 75, 106–8; level of, 28, 30–1, 36–7, 39–40, 46, 48, 100; nineteenth century attitude, 46–8, 50, 75–6; pregnant women, 41–2; Tudor period, 27–36; types, 27; *see also* clergy (benefit of), property offences
Capper, John, 52
Carpenter, Mary, 79
carting, 21–2, 47, 48, 49
Cason, Joan, 34
Castlereagh, Viscount, 46
Chatham prison, 73
Children and Young Persons Act (1969), 119

Christie, John, 105
Churchill, Winston, 16, 98
Clarke, Terence, 107
Clemmer, Donald, 93
clergy, benefit of, 23, 27, 40–1, 42
Clerkenwell House of Correction, 68, 74
Cockburn, J. S., 41–2
Coggan, Geoff, 123
Community Service Orders, 118, 127, 130
confessions, 34
convicts, 50, 51–61, 70
corporal punishment, 76–8, 119, *see also* flogging, whipping
crank, the, 72, 89
crime rate, 30–1, 85, 103, 128–9
Criminal Justice Acts, 99, 105, 119–20
Cubitt, William, 72
Cudmore, Thomas, 25
custodial punishment, *see* prison

Dartmoor prison, 72, 87, 99, 112, 114
de Lacy, Margaret, 86, 87
death penalty, *see* capital punishment
Denman, Thomas, first Baron, 79
detention centres, 109, 119, 128
deterrence, 6–9, 127
Devon, 20, 30, 46
Discharged Prisoners' Aid Society, 84
Dodge, Calvert R., 121
drawing and quartering, 27
drunkenness, 20, 83, 91
Du Cane, Edmund, 66–7, 74, 89
ducking stool, 19–20
Dülmen, Richard van, 36
Durham prison, 112, 114
Durkheim, Emil, 13

Eardley-Wilmot, Sir John Eardley, 57
ecclesiastical courts, 22
Ede, Chuter, 119
Education Act (1876), 80
electronic tagging, 124
Elias, Norbert, 129
Ellis, Ruth, 106
embezzlement, 20, 82
Essex, 20, 21, 29, 31, 39, 41
Evans, Timothy, 105
evidence, laws of, 35
Ewart, William, 103
excommunication, 22
executions, public, 6–7, 19, 31–5, 49, 51

Feltham institution, 94
Fielding, Henry, 44
fines, 1–2, 19, 24–5, 91, 99
Fitzsimmonds, Joshua, 45
Fleet prison, 68
flogging: armed forces, 76; convicts, 67, 73, 99; nineteenth century, 76–8; vagrants, 77–8; *see also* whipping
Floyd, William, 57
forgery, 46–7
Foucault, Michel, 51, 69, 75, 82, 86–7, 98, 129
Fox, Sir Lionel, 111
fraud, 82

Gallup Polls, 122
Gaol Act (1823), 84
gaolers, *see* prison officers
garrotting, 76–7, 78, 106
Germany, 36, 110, 121
Ghent, Maison de Force, 44, 62
Gibson, Thomas, 44
Gladstone Committee, 67, 74, 75, 85, 90, 93–4, 96, 111
Gladstone, Herbert, 67
Gloucester prison, 62, 99
Goodcole, Henry, 32
Greenway, Francis Howard, 60

Halifax, 27
Hanawalt, Barbara, 28
hanging, 27, 28, 31, 127

hard labour, 51–2, 67, 99
Hawkins, D. J. B., 13
Hay, Douglas, 38–9
Henderson, Edmund, 66
Hobhouse, Stephen, 90, 96
Holford Committee, 63
Holker, Sir John, 103
Holland, Dorothy, 55
Hollande, Elizabeth, 22
Hollis, Christopher, 105
homicide, 7, 28, *see also* murder
Homicide Act (1957), 106–7
Hood, Roger, 95
Horsham gaol, 62
houses of correction, 25–6, 44–5, 49, 61
Howard, John, 44, 61–2, 67–9, 87, 122, 127
Howard League for Penal Reform, 106
Hudson, John, 55
hulks, the, 51–4, 60, 87, 127, 129; guards, 53

Ignatieff, Michael, 51, 64, 65, 75, 82
Ilive, Jacob, 68–9, 74
Immigration Act, 3
Industrial Schools Act (1857), 80
infanticide, 37, 76
insanity as a defence, 76
Interregnum, 18, 35, 37
Isloppe, Jane, 22

Jebb, Sir Joshua, 64, 66
Jenkins, Roy, 112
Jones, Howard, 96

Kant, Immanuel, 6
Kellerhals, Otto, 92
King, Peter, 39
Koestler, Arthur, 106

larceny, 46–7, 78, 82, *see also* robbery, theft
Leicester prison, 112
Lewis, C. S., 11
Lewis, Frank D., 55
literacy, 23, 40, 83
London, 21, 30, 36–7, 50, 55, 61
Lorton reformatory, 92
Lowdham Grange, 95

Mackintosh, Sir James, 46
M'Naghten, Daniel, 76
Macquarie, Lachlan, 60
magistrates, 83–4
Maidstone prison, 99
Marine Society, 78
Marxism, 15, 129, 130
Massie, Joseph, 45
mercy, 38, 76
Middlesex, 21–2, 29, 36–7, 50
Millbank prison, 63, 64, 66, 73–4
Mitchell, Frank, 112
Moberley, Sir Walter, 10
Molesworth Committee, 57–8, 59, 61, 64
Morris, William Douglas, 67
Mountbatten Report, 112–13
murder, 27, 37, 101, *see also* homicide
Murder (Abolition of the Death Penalty) Bill (1964), 107
mutilation, 21

National Council for the Abolition of the Death Penalty, 104, 106
National Union of Police and Prison Officers, 98
Netherlands, 102, 110, 121
New Hall Camp, 92
New South Wales, 54, 58–60
New South Wales Corps, 56
Newgate prison, 22, 68
Nield, James, 65
Nokes, Peter, 126

oakum, picking, 71
Offences Against the Person Act (1861), 75
Official Secrets Act, 122
open prisons, 92–3, 109
outlaws, 28

Paley, Reverend William, 38, 49
pardons, 38–40
Parkhurst Gaol, 64, 79, 87, 96
Paterson, Sir Alexander, 90, 92, 94–5, 111–12
Paul, Sir George Onesiphorus, 62, 87
Pease, J. W., 103
Peel, Sir Robert, 47
Penal Reform League, 104
Penal Servitude Act (1865), 66
penance, 22–3, 48
Pentonville prison, 64, 65, 66, 82, 87, 127
Perkins, William, 33
Philanthropic Society, 78, 79
Phillip, Captain Arthur, 55–6
pillory, 21, 47, 127
poaching, 26
Pointing, John, 121
Portland prison, 72, 94
poverty, 25–6, 83
power, 15, 51, 86
pregnancy, plea of, 41–2
Prevention of Crime Act (1908), 90, 94, 96
preventive detention, 96
prison: American systems, 64–5, 92–3, 94; central/local government, 63–4, 65–6; classification of prisoners, 67; comparisons abroad, 110, 121; cost, 3–4, 91–2, 109; dispersal, 109, 114; effectiveness debates, 4, 126; eighteenth century, 44–6, 49, 61–3; escapes, 112, 124; houses of correction, 25–6, 44–5, 49, 61; legislation, 64, 66–8, 73, 84, 89, 99; levels of imprisonment, 110–11; literature, 68–70; nineteenth century, 50, 63–75, 81–3, 85, 88; officers, 25, 61, 73–4, 89, 93, 97–8, 109, 114–16, 124; open, 92–3, 109; overcrowding, 109–10; privatization, 124; recidivists, 81–3, 96, 111; riots, 73, 99, 122, 124; security, 112–14; solitary confinement, 65, 73, 127; statistics, 2–3, 67, 73, 80, 82–3, 85, 90–1, 109–10, 119; Tudor/Stuart, 25–6; twentieth century, 2, 90–9; work, 71–2, 89
Prison Acts, 68, 73, 89, 90
Prison Commission(ers), 64, 73, 90, 91, 98, 111–12
Prison Department, 112, 113
Prison Officers' Association (POA), 98, 113, 114, 116, 127
Prison Officers' Representative Board, 98
prisoners: classification of, 67, 69; discharged, 84–5; dispersal of, 113; risk categories, 112–13
Probation of First Offenders Act (1886), 81
probation service, 81, 96–7, 99, 116–18, 127
property offences, 7, 30–1, 35, 38, 46, 55, 78, 125
prostitution, 21, 77–8, 83
public opinion, 48, 64, 67, 108, 121–2, 127
punishment: attitudes to, 16, 126; deterrent, 6–9, 127; early modern, 19–27; hard labour, 51–2, 67, 99; imprisonment, *see* houses of correction, hulks, prison; public discussion, 18, *see also* public opinion; reformative, 9–13, 48, 63, 69, 79, 127; retributive, 12–14, 77; search for secondary, 36–49; shaming, 19, 47–9; *see also* public opinion, capital punishment, corporal punishment, transportation

Radzinowicz Committee, 113
Rawlinson, Sir Peter, 107
receiving stolen goods, 82
recidivists, 81–3, 96, 111, 127
reform of convicted criminals, 9–13, 48, 63, 69, 79, 127
Reformatory Movement, 79

Reformatory Schools Act (1854), 80
release on licence, 99
religious offences, 28
remand centres, 109
remission for good conduct, 97, 99
Richmond, Charles Lennox, third Duke of, 62, 87
robbery, 27, 77, *see also* larceny, theft
Robinson, Michael Massey, 60
Rome, house of correction, 44
Romilly, Sir Samuel, 45–6
Royal Commissions on Capital Punishment, 8, 103, 105
Ruggles-Brise, Sir Evelyn, 90, 94

scaffold rituals, 31–5
scolds, 19–20
Scudder, Kenyon, 93
Scull, Andrew, 121
Security from Violence Act, 77
sentencing policy, 1–3, 29–31, 82–4, 121
servants, 26, 27, 28
sex offences, 21, 28
'short sharp shock', 119, 128
Silverman, Sydney, 105, 106
Sing Sing prison system, 65
skimmington, rituals of, 19
Smith, Sir Thomas, 40
social work, 81
solitary confinement, 65, 73, 127
speeches from the gallows, 31–5
Spierenburg, Pieter, 129–30
Stanley, Stephen, 121
Stern, Vivien, 114
stocks, the, 19, 20, 47, 48, 49
stolen goods, value of, 24, 42, 83
suspended, sentences, 1, 117–18

Taverner, Samuel, 81–2
Temple, William, 105
theft, 20, 23–4, 26, *see also* larceny, robbery
Theft Act (1968), 9
Thomas, J. E., 125
Thoresby, Ralph, 34
traitors, 27, 32
transportation, 42–4, 45, 49, 51–61, 125, 127, 129
Transportation Act (1718), 43
Transportation, Committee on, 53
treadwheel, the, 72, 74, 87, 89, 127
treason, law of, 27
Tyburn, 19, 31, 34, 36

Ullathorne, William, 58
Underdown, David, 20
United States of America, 14, 102–3, 121, 124

vagrancy, 23, 25–6, 77–8, 83
Vagrancy Amendment Act (1898), 77
van der Elst, Violet, 104
Van Diemen's Land, 54–9, 64
Vaux, James Hardy, 53

Wakefield prison, 82–3, 92
Walker, Martin, 122
Wandsworth prison, 112
Warwickshire, 25, 28
Weber, Max, 130
whipping, 23–4, 42, 76
Whitbread, Samuel, 84
Whitelaw, William, 128
Wilson, Charles, 112
witchcraft, 20, 28, 34
Wood, Stuart, 71

York Castle county gaol, 44
young offenders: eighteenth-century treatment, 52, 57, 126; nineteenth-century treatment, 58, 76, 78–81, 83, 126; twentieth-century treatment, 1, 109, 118–20, 124, 126, 128; *see also* borstal system
Young, Robert, 78
youth custody centres, 109, 119